Tarragon Island

by Nikki Tate

Sono Nis Press

VICTORIA, BRITISH COLUMBIA

Text copyright © 1999 by Nikki Tate
Cover illustration copyright © 1999 by Ljuba Levstek

Canadian Cataloguing in Publication Data

Tate, Nikki, 1962-
   Tarragon Island

   ISBN 1-55039-103-8
   I. Title.
PS8589.A8735T27 1999   jC813".54   C99-911036-5
PS7.T2113Ta 1999

We acknowledge the support of the Canada Council
for the Arts for our publishing program.
We acknowledge the assistance of the Province of British Columbia,
through the British Columbia Arts Council.

All quotations are from the following sources:
The Writer's Quotation Book: A Literary Companion,
edited by James Charlton, Penguin Books, 1986.

Bartlett's Familiar Quotations, Sixteenth Edition,
General Editor Justin Keplan, Little, Brown & Company, 1992.

Cover design by Jim Brennan

Published by
SONO NIS PRESS
PO Box 5550, Stn. B
Victoria, BC V8R 6S4
tel: (250) 598-7807
sono.nis@islandnet.com
http://www.islandnet.com/sononis/

Distributed in the U.S. by
Orca Book Publishers
Box 468
Custer, WA 98240-0468
1-800-210-5277

PRINTED AND BOUND IN CANADA BY KROMAR PRINTING

For Mom (the Word Lady),
whose enthusiasm for language is contagious.
Without your persistent corrections I'd still
be misusing the dative case.

And for Dad,
with thanks for those rare and treasured
peeks into your studio.

Acknowledgements

Tarragon Island would not have been the same book without the invaluable help of many. A huge thank you to Ann West who is simply a fantastic editor—I don't know where I'd be without her wise and thoughtful suggestions. I could not ask for a more supportive publisher than Diane Morriss at Sono Nis Press—her unflagging encouragement and enthusiasm have made it possible to realize my dream of becoming a novelist. Maddy, Joey, Caitlin, Ellie, and Frieda provided excellent feedback on the manuscript—thank you for taking the time to read the draft and then answer all those questions! Dolce, my cockatiel, sat on my shoulder as I wrote this book. Her cheerful company and sense of humour (she likes to dance on the keyboard and chase my fingers as I type) kept me smiling through the long and difficult job of writing a book. And finally, thank you to Danielle who has been so patient with me! I know how you hate the look of my closed office door and dread the words, "I'm in the middle of revisions." Without your input and assistance when Heather had incurable writer's block, *Tarragon Island* may never have been finished.

Author's note

The Gulf Islands are located between Vancouver, British Columbia and Vancouver Island. Anyone who has taken the ferry from Tsawwassen to Swartz Bay will be familiar with the general location of the fictional Tarragon Island. Years ago I was lucky enough to have lived on Saltspring Island. My memories of island life helped fill in the background details of *Tarragon Island*.

Chapter One

Collected Quote #1
Most of the basic material a writer works with is acquired
before the age of fifteen.—Willa Cather
Source: Mrs. Thompson, Grade 5 teacher

My life is a complete disaster. How hard can that be to understand?

"Mom, I don't want to live on this stupid island! Why can't we move back to Toronto?"

"Heather. You are twelve years old. You have your whole life ahead of you. When you grow up, you can live wherever you want."

My mother obviously has no idea how bad things are. Actually, I think she understands perfectly well. She just doesn't want to admit she was wrong to drag us all here.

Mom looks away from me for a second to unplug the kettle and I stick my tongue out at her. She turns back to say something else and catches me.

Her face irons itself into calm. This is her angry face and the voice that goes with it is quiet.

"If you know what's good for you, you won't say another word."

My open mouth is dry and filled with half-formed words.

"Heather." Mom's voice is a little gentler. "I know how hard this move has been on you, but that's still no excuse for talking back and being rude."

Her kind voice is even harder to take than her anger of a moment ago.

I don't want to hear any more and I sure don't trust myself to say anything polite. My cheeks heat up as the first hot tears waver in my eyes.

I try to count to ten under my breath, the way Mom says I should when I'm mad. But before I can get to three the tears spill over and I bolt down the hall and out the back door.

I run past Mia, our Yorkshire terrier who is sunning herself on the back steps, dodge around Matt's wagon loaded high with bits of driftwood, fumble with the latch on the gate because I can't see at all now. All I can think about is getting away: away from my mother, away from my new house, away from everything! I keep running across the field behind the house even though my legs start to feel wobbly and heavy at the same time, like when something in a dream chases me and I can't move a muscle.

Except this isn't a dream. This is my nightmare life.

My life wasn't always awful. In fact, until three weeks ago, it was basically great. Three weeks ago we lived in Toronto, in a great old house that was only a two-minute walk from The Village Bookshop. I still remember the first time Dad took me to the "Old VB," as he called it.

"Heather, there probably won't be any other children at the poetry reading, so you'll have to sit quietly, even if you get bored."

I was about nine at the time and Dad had seen a notice in the paper: "Young Voices: Green Visions. Poetry by young people about nature."

By the time he saw that ad and decided I might

like to go, since I was almost a "Young Person" myself, he and Mom had already covered our whole entire fridge with my poems. Even though the spelling is terrible and some of them don't make any sense, I packed every last one when we moved here to Tarragon Island. Dad said that's what writers do— they collect everything "for posterity."

When he said that, I didn't know what the heck he was talking about. The only time I'd heard a word like *posterity* was when Mom said, "Stop teasing Mia or I'll swat your posterior!" so at first I thought he was making a rude joke.

Now I know that real, serious writers keep everything just in case they ever get famous and people want to know how they got started. Take me, for example. I wrote my first poem when I was four. That's technically before I could actually write.

One morning I woke up very early. I told Dad that the clouds looked like they were on fire, like flames were tickling the belly of the sky. He got all excited and made me say it again and then he wrote the words down for me. When Mom came into the kitchen he read it to her three times and then stuck it up on the fridge so we'd never forget there was a poet in the house.

After that, I started paying attention to how things looked and sounded and felt and smelled and then I'd tell Dad and he'd write the words down for me.

So, by the time he invited me to go to the nature poetry reading, I'd been writing poetry for five years and I'd branched out into stories and puppet plays, too.

Dad and I sure loved the Old VB. It was a little bookstore owned by a guy called Charlie O'Neil. The place had a gazillion books piled up to the ceiling, books in boxes, fancy old books in glass cases, brand new books at the front of the store, used books in the back, big, shiny volumes with beautiful photographs on their covers in the window, and even stacks of books on the counter where you paid. Toko, the store's black cat, slept right on top of the reading armchair at the front of the store. When I sat down to read, he reached down from his perch and stroked my head with his paw.

Charlie knew where every single book was hiding and he never minded if sometimes I sat in the armchair and read all afternoon without buying a thing.

"Where would we be without books?" He waved his hand up towards the very top shelves that he could reach only with his rolling wooden ladder. "And where would I be without book people like you?"

He didn't care that I was just a kid. Right from the first time we met, we got along great. I think he was impressed that I sat still for so long, listening to those nature poets. I didn't ever tell Dad, but most of it was really boring. The best part was one skinny teenager with frizzy black hair who did this poem called "Brook Babble." She didn't use any words at all! She made all these watery noises with her lips and in her throat and when I closed my eyes it sounded like there was a stream burbling through the bookshop.

What was most amazing was that she had a piece of paper in front of her and she kept looking down at it, as if she could read the sounds she made. I'd have given anything to know how to spell all those gurgling, splishing, glugging noises, but when she was done, she folded away her paper and stuck it in a soft leather pouch that hung around her neck.

After that, whenever famous writers came to the store to read their poems or parts out of their novels,

8

Charlie always made sure to invite me to come along and listen.

"If you're ever going to be a decent writer, Blake, you have to read and listen to real authors," he said, using my last name like he always did. Which is how I got to meet Marion Alsworthy. Charlie said it was a chance in a lifetime and called Ms. Alsworthy a "literary icon." I had no idea what an "icon" did, but I was sure impressed when Charlie piled all the books she had written on the round display table at the front of the store.

"Try reading this one: *A Prairie Girl at Noon*. I think you'll like it."

The book was pretty fat and had quite small writing, but after about two chapters I got right into it and couldn't put it down, not even at the dinner table, which made Mom mad. I'll tell you how good a writer Marion Alsworthy is. When I reached the part where the prairie girl has to stand at her best friend's graveside, I cried. And I almost never cry when I'm reading. She just made it so real I felt like I was right there at the funeral burying my best friend. That's my dream, to write beautiful stories that make people cry.

The Old VB was packed to the rafters the night Marion Alsworthy came to read from her new collection of poems, *Winter Bliss and Summer Solitude*. When she was finished reading, Charlie introduced us.

"This is Blake," he said. "Good name for a writer, don't you think?"

Even though so many people had come to listen to her read and lots of them were lined up clutching copies of her books so she could sign them, she leaned close to me and asked what I was writing at the moment.

I couldn't believe it. Marion Alsworthy wanted to know about *my* work!

"Well, I have a poem in my pocket." Right away I felt stupid and wished I hadn't said anything. What kind of a dope carries poetry around in her pocket?

"May I see it?"

She smiled at me, a wide, dazzling, friendly smile, one that said, "Of course you have a poem in your pocket."

She smoothed the paper on the table in front of her, pushing a pile of her own books to the side to make more room. Her thin, elegant fingers stroked the page as she read, caressing my work as if it were the most beautiful thing she had ever seen in the world.

"You have real promise, Blake," she said. "You might want to look at this line here, though—it's a bit awkward. 'When once I dreamed of fine cuisine . . .'"

When she read the line aloud I wanted to crawl under the table and never come out—it sounded so dumb, even though the whole poem was about kitchens and a girl who disobeys her mother and gets burned by touching a hot frying pan.

"There's lots of dramatic tension in this part . . . do you write anything else? Fiction?"

"I'm working on a novel." I blurted it out, so embarrassed by that point it didn't matter what I said.

It sounded crazy. I was only eleven at the time. Who would take a kid like me seriously?

"I wrote my first novel when I was eleven," she said, flashing her brilliant smile at me again. "You must let me know when you have your first book signing. I'd love to come."

I've thought a lot about that day. Inviting Marion Alsworthy to the launch of my first novel makes perfect sense. I already know how I'm going to start my speech.

"My road to success would not have been possible without the help of some very special people, especially Marion Alsworthy, one of Canada's finest poets and novelists."

When I say that, she'll nod graciously from her seat in the front row and we'll exchange knowing smiles.

At least, it used to be clear that's how it would go. Marion Alsworthy lives in Toronto so it would have been easy for her to attend my book launch, if only we hadn't moved.

But now that we don't live anywhere near Toronto, there's no way Marion Alsworthy or anyone else important will ever come to hear me read. We didn't just move to the suburbs, we moved clear across the country to a ridiculous little island in British Columbia. Tarragon Island. An island thirty-seven kilometres long, shaped like a pear, and named after an herb, if you can believe it!

The closest city is Victoria, which is so small it's hardly a real city at all. Besides, getting off this rock is a lot of trouble. We have to drive to the ferry (there isn't even a bus here!), wait forever for the next boat, travel nearly an hour to the terminal on Vancouver Island, and then drive for an hour to get to the little place they call "downtown." What a joke. Victoria is nothing compared to a *real* downtown like they have in Toronto.

I don't have a hope of ever meeting another real writer again.

Chapter Two

Collected Quote #28
However great a man's natural talent may be, the art of writing cannot be learned all at once.
—Jean Jacques Rousseau
Source: Dad when he was trying to comfort me the first time the kitchen poem was rejected

"Heather?"

It's easier than you'd think to hide in a tree. I'm not even very high up but Matt hasn't spotted me yet. I have noticed that most people when they walk look straight ahead or down at the ground. Matt is definitely a "down at the ground" kind of person. That's because he's a collector.

"Heather?"

He doesn't actually sound very interested in finding me. If he really wanted to get my attention, he'd yell louder. A breeze ruffles through the leaves and the pages of my notebook flutter. Matt has stopped to look at something beside the altar. Well, it's not really an altar. It's a big flat boulder, big enough that I can sit on it and rest my notebook in front of me to write. It reminds me of a place in Narnia where the lion, Aslan, hangs out. *The Lion, the Witch and the Wardrobe* is one of my favourite books. I've read it four times.

I was sitting on the altar earlier but it got too hot in the sun, so I moved up here into the maple tree. Matt is really staring at something. A sick feeling filters into the pit of my stomach. *Maybe I left a page of my notebook down there? Or the letter I was writing to Maggie? Maybe that's what's so interesting?*

Holding my elbows close to my sides, and being very careful not to let the paper make any noise, I turn the pages of my notebook. My breath seeps out with a sigh. All the pages are still here and Maggie's letter is tucked in at the back.

Matt stretches out his arm and picks something up off the ground. He turns it over in his hands and then carefully puts it into his pocket.

I hate doing the laundry when Matt's clothes are involved. Mom taught me I always have to check the pockets so I don't wash anything important. Or messy. Messy is much more likely in Matt's case.

Once I found a bird's wing in his pocket and another time some dead leaves. Rocks, shells, and feathers are normal. His room looks like a museum. Every possible surface in our Toronto house was covered with his treasures. A hornet's nest, a tiny skull with long pointy front teeth, an owl's feather. I don't know why Mom let him pack all that junk. Moving was a perfect opportunity to get rid of it.

His pets are another story. When he had his hamster-breeding business, he had eleven hamsters in his room. The problem was, every hamster had to have its own cage. I found that out the hard way when one time I saw one of his long-haired, smoke-grey teddy bear hamsters wandering around in the hallway. I thought I was doing Matt a favour when I rescued the hamster and put it into the cage closest to Matt's bedroom door.

About an hour later I heard Matt upstairs,

screaming, "Mom! Help!" and then these weird whistles and shrieks.

I ran up the stairs after Mom. Matt shot out of his bedroom yelling, "Stop the massacre! Quick! Tiny's gonna get killed!"

The two hamsters tumbled around, squeaking and biting each other. Matt grabbed a ruler from his desk and thrust it at Mom. She poked it into the cage to separate Puff and Tiny, who really did seem intent on killing each other.

They jumped apart and quick as anything, Mom scooped Tiny out of the cage and handed him to Matt. Tiny's little sides heaved in and out and there were several bald patches where Puff had ripped his fur out.

Gently, Matt stroked Tiny's head with his thumb and inspected him thoroughly. "I don't see any blood," he said.

Mom patted Matt's arm. "Good thing you were at home and heard them fighting. How on earth did they get in together?"

Both Matt and Mom looked at me. "Tiny was loose in the hall . . . I didn't think it mattered, which cage . . ."

"Everyone knows hamsters are very territorial," Matt said and carefully put Tiny back in his own cage by the window.

Since Matt loves rodents and birds so much (he also has four cockatiels and a budgie called Sigmund), it's kind of a surprise that he likes the cats, Tony and Mathilde, as much as he does.

Maybe it's because the cats are useful when it comes to adding bits and pieces of wild animals to Matt's museum collection. That's where he got the bird's wing. If you ask me, it's disgusting to take apart dead animals and then display their bones and skulls and feathers. Unfortunately, Mom is no help. She's a veterinarian and when she wants to be revolting, she tells stories about the things vets dissect when they go to college. Matt and Mom understand each other.

Me, I bury dead things. Behind our old house I turned a small corner of the lawn into a graveyard. If the cats brought me a "present," I'd find a box, line it with paper towel and then bury the dead bird or mouse. I named all the animals whose spirits had passed away. I marked their graves with little piles of stones and wrote down the burial dates in my notebook.

Bliss Harrington—House Sparrow—March 11.

Matt never knew what happened to his bird wing, the one I found in his pocket when I was doing the laundry. I didn't feel right naming a body part, so that day I wrote,

Wing of Freedom—Russet with Gold Flecks—April 23.

So far, nothing dead has turned up on Tarragon Island, so I haven't made a new graveyard yet. In fact, I don't think I'll bother since I'm going to run away anyhow. Nobody asked me if I wanted to move here, so I'm not going to tell anyone I'm leaving. I phoned the bus company and found out a kid's one-way bus ticket to Guelph, Ontario costs seventy-five dollars. If I can save up that much, I can escape from here.

Great literature is filled with stories of people who escape—like the Count of Monte Cristo, who gets away from his prison tower by pretending to be dead. I figure I'll escape by taking a bus all the way to my grandparents' big farm outside Guelph. By the time I get there, Granny and Grandpa will be so glad to see me they won't care if I stay for a while. And, once they find out how useful I am, they'll let me stay, maybe forever. I'll write about my experiences as a twelve-year-old runaway and lots of people will buy my book. Maybe someone will even want to make a movie.

"Heather!"

I jump so hard when Dad calls, my notebook falls out of the tree.

"There you are. Matt said he looked all over for you. Didn't you hear him calling?"

"Ouch!" I decide not to answer so I don't have to lie. My foot is stuck in a fork of the tree and I grab onto the trunk tighter, trying to scramble free.

"Come on down from there!"

"I'm trying!"

I wiggle my foot until it pops out from between the branches and then swing down onto the grass beside Dad.

"Careful!"

Mia's lying sprawled in the long grass and I nearly land right on top of her. She rolls over but doesn't bother to get up. She just stretches and looks at me sideways, hoping to get her tummy scratched.

"You dropped this," Dad says.

He holds my notebook out to me and I snatch it quickly. Dad's not the kind of person to read other people's notebooks, but still, since I had just finished writing about how much I think Dad has changed since we moved here, I don't want him to see any of it by accident.

For one thing, Dad has developed this obsession with sailboats. I don't get it. Dad isn't really the outdoorsy type. It's no secret it was mostly Mom's idea to move here. You see, I heard some of their conversations before we moved because I had discovered that sound travelled really clearly from the living room, up the heating vent, and into the upstairs bathroom. If I sat up there quietly, I could hear everything they said, and since they were planning on dragging me along, I figured I had a right to know what was going on.

Mom was the one who grew up on a farm, and she's the one who wanted to live in the country again so she could be a vet to farm animals and not just to city pets like cats and dogs and iguanas. During the six months before we actually moved, Mom made several trips out here to supervise the renovations to the house, find out about schools, and let people know a new vet was coming to town to replace Dr. Wong who was retiring. Once she had made up her mind, she could hardly wait to get out of Toronto. At the end, she left us behind to finish packing up the Toronto house and she came here to organize the vet clinic, hire Milly (the lady who works part-time as Mom's receptionist), and make sure the house was ready in time for our arrival.

Living in the country is fine for people like Matt and Mom who are quite happy spending their days talking to things with scales and feathers and wagging tails, but for artists like me and Dad, we need all the excitement of a big city. At least, I thought that's what Dad wanted.

The last art show he had in Toronto, all his work showed how people live in cities. The paintings were crowded and colourful and one guy who writes for the *Toronto Sun* said they were the "noisiest" paintings he had ever seen.

I worry about Dad because it's very quiet here, especially since we don't even live in Rosehip, the little village on Tarragon Island. We live on twenty acres out in the middle of the country. We can't see the ocean from where we live because our farm is in a valley surrounded by hills. Since this is an island, the water's never far away and Dad spends a lot of time riding his bike to the marina where he keeps his little sailboat, *Ariel*.

There's something very strange about Dad and that boat. From the first time I remember Mom talking about moving, Dad started talking about boats.

"I could get a boat, couldn't I?"

The way he said it was like he was daring someone to stop him. And sure enough, the very first week after we arrived, he phoned a guy who had an ad in the *Tarragon Times* and bought this little old twenty-four-foot sailboat called *Ariel*.

In fact, I'm kind of surprised to see Dad standing under my tree because he has been spending most days down at the boat. I don't think he's even painted a single picture since *Ariel* came into his life.

"Are you busy, Heather?"

How can I answer that? Of course I'm busy, I'm writing. But nobody around here seems to understand that writing is my life's work and that if I don't get going on my novel, it won't write itself.

Luckily, Dad doesn't wait for me to answer. "I was thinking you need a place to work."

"Work?"

"Write. You know, a special place you could go to work on your . . . novel."

This is also pretty suspicious. Dad is not the building type. He might be a very good artist, but he's lousy with a hammer. So is Mom, for that matter. That's another reason why we never should have left Toronto. Back at the old house when something needed fixing, we called Grandpa. Between the two of them, he and Granny can fix just about anything.

"You want to build something?"

"Not exactly from scratch. Follow me."

Chapter Three

Collected Quote #55
Most writers are in a state of gloom a good deal of the time; they need perpetual reassurance.
—John Hall Wheelock
Source: Charlie when he gave me a copy of the book
You, Too, Can Write a Great Novel

A few minutes later when Dad and Mia and I are standing in front of the old chicken coop, it's all I can do to speak without being rude. "You're kidding, right?"

"No, I'm not kidding. Every writer needs a place to write. Somewhere private. Somewhere quiet."

"Somewhere inspiring would be nice."

"Heather, use your imagination. If we clean this out, slap on a coat of paint, find a little desk for you . . . look, there's even a window."

Mia yelps and plunges through the thick tangle of weeds into the open door of the chicken coop. Her high-pitched frantic barking is unmistakable—she is definitely on the trail of something! Our Toronto lapdog has been transformed into a wild hunter. Something long and dark scurries out of the shadowy interior with Mia in hot pursuit. She yips and yelps and whines and tries desperately to squeeze under the building to follow her prey.

"What was that?" I ask, hoping to convince

myself it might have been a rabbit, or at worst, a squirrel.

"Looked like a rat to me."

"Ugghh. That's great—a rat-infested chicken coop."

Mia races around to the back of the coop but can't get close because of the thick tangle of blackberry canes engulfing the shed.

"This is an old farm—you have to expect a few rats. They'll move out when you move in. A couple of good clean-up sessions and you won't know the place."

Part of me wants to tell Dad not to go to a lot of trouble since I'm not going to be around for long anyway, but another part of me thinks that while I'm waiting to save up enough money for my bus ticket to Ontario, it would be kind of cool to have a real writing cottage, my own workshop. Dad's right. When we clean the place out the rats will probably leave since the cats will be able to come in, and . . .

This is one of the drawbacks of having a very good imagination. I'm already looking at the saggy roof and missing planks of the old chicken house and calling the ramshackle outbuilding a writing cottage.

Mia yelps and streaks off through the grassy field and disappears into the trees. I hope she's chased the rat away.

"Okay," I say, playing along. "Can I pick the paint colours?"

I don't give him a chance to say no. "Mauve. With white trim. No, black. Black trim." I squint until the edges of the coop are very clear and I can't see the filth, the cobwebs masking the window, the thick mass of blackberry canes that have grown as high as the roof.

It makes me think of Quote #6 in my collection

that has something to do with "a room of one's own." Charlie found it for me when he heard I was collecting quotes about writers. It came from Virginia Woolf, another famous author, who said that every writer needs a place to work. This is more like a coop of one's own, but I guess it's better than a pigsty.

At the hardware store, I have a vivid hallucination. Don't get me wrong, I'm not crazy or anything. But it seems like just about every time I come to Rosehip, I think I see someone I used to know in Toronto.

Today is no exception. Dad has sent me into the hardware store to choose the paint for my writing coop.

"It's easy. Just pick out the colour you like."

Easy? I've just picked up my fourth can of paint to read the label when I see Jenny McIntosh pass by the end of the paint aisle.

I run to the end of the aisle and look both ways. It *is* her! Nobody else in the world has hair the same colour as she does. It's actually two different shades, a silvery blonde on top and light brown underneath. And Jenny always wears brightly coloured hair clips high on both sides of her head, clips that barely catch any hair at all.

I go all the way up to where Jenny is standing in line at the cashier. *She must be asking for directions to my place! She's come to visit me! Won't she be surprised when she finds out I'm standing right behind her?*

"Anything else for you?"

"No, thank you." I freeze. The voice is different. Nothing like Jenny's at all. And this girl is buying a nozzle for a hose. Jenny would have no use for something like that.

"May I help you?"

"No. No—I'm just . . . buying paint."

The woman at the register flicks her cash drawer shut.

"Actually, do you know anything about paint?" I wish Dad had told me more about what I should be buying. Just because he's an expert on paint doesn't mean I am, too.

"A bit—what do you need?"

"Something to paint a . . . small cottage."

The woman follows me back to the paint. I feel a kind of helpless grin freezing on my face. "I didn't know there were so many kinds of paint."

"You need a good exterior-quality latex."

"Where are the different colours?" I ask.

"Unless you are looking for these standard colours, I have to mix some for you. Just pick the colour closest to what you want on these cards here."

She points at a rack that has thousands of strips of coloured paper. "Midnight blue. Cobalt blue. Adriatic blue. Adonis blue. Bluebell blue. Deep Sea blue." There are at least two hundred shades of blue. Maybe more.

I start looking through the rows and rows of colour strips. Too pink. Too red. Too dark. Too purple. Too wishy washy. Too electric.

My hallucination about Jenny makes me think of my very best friend in the whole world. That's Maggie—Mags for short. She decorates and redecorates her room for fun. Mags would know about paint colours. If she lived here, we could pick out the paint together.

Clutching a handful of coloured paper strips I freeze with a kind of sadness I didn't know a person could feel in the middle of a hardware store. It seems more like the feeling you should get at a funeral, or when your dog gets run over. A lady walks behind me and reaches for a can of paint on the top shelf, then changes her mind and puts it back.

I wish she would go away because I bet she can

hear my funny breathing and is probably wondering why a girl is standing in the paint aisle looking like she's going to cry. She chooses another can of paint and then moves away.

"Are you finding what you want?" I have nearly forgotten about the hardware clerk who has been tidying rolls of masking tape and hanging all the paint brushes in their proper places.

"No!" I blurt it out and she looks a bit surprised. "I mean, there are just so many colours."

She nods and gives me an understanding look. I force myself to ignore my blushing, my dizziness, and my pounding heart and get back to looking at the paint strips.

I'm getting closer—the hues are softer now—pale pastel pinks, delicate mauves, and soft lilacs. Perfect!

I hold up the strip of paper. "Summer Lilac." My voice is almost normal, not weepy like I thought it would be.

"I'll take two tins of this colour—Summer Lilac," I say, trying to sound calm.

The clerk tips her head to one side and says, "Don't worry, dear. If you don't like how the colour turns out, you can always paint over it."

I have to smile at that! Maybe some people get so worked up about paint colours that they cry in the hardware store. As the clerk squirts tint into the cans and mixes the paint, I imagine a dramatic scene in the paint aisle.

"Oh, Pansy! My kitchen walls are revolting! How could I have painted them yucky olive green? My husband hates it so much he's going to leave me and the children penniless!"

"Don't cry, Briony. I fully support your decision to try again. How about this cheerful yellow?"

Briony collapses to the floor, knocking over the

masking tape stand. Rolls of masking tape tumble down the aisle.

"Yellow? Never!" Briony gasps, clutching at her throat.

"What's wrong with yellow?" Pansy asks her dearest friend.

"That was the colour of my mother's dress at . . ." Sob. Sob. ". . . the dress she was buried in after a long, dreadful battle with leukemia . . ."

"I said, would you like a bag?"

"Oh, sorry." The clerk is starting to look very worried about me.

"No! I mean, I can just take the cans like this."

I pay and flee. The paint companies should name their brightest red after me. "Heather's Burning Blush." I bet it would be a popular colour for little red wagons.

Chapter Four

Collected Quote #14
There is only one trait that marks the writer. He is always watching. It's a kind of trick of the mind and he's born with it.—Morley Callaghan
Source: Charlie when he told me the best way to write good dialogue is to spy on other people's conversations

Girl Next Door—Observations
Small. Skinny legs. Way skinnier than I am. And shorter. And her hair is a bit longer than mine and much lighter. I keep thinking my hair will get lighter brown because I'm in the sun so much but it's not happening. This girl's hair is straight, not wavy like mine.

I can only see the girl's skinny legs when she runs because she always wears long dresses. Rags, really. She looks like a girl from a novel by Charles Dickens, someone who would have worked in a poorhouse. Her dresses aren't ripped or anything like that. It's more like they belong to somebody else bigger—a sister or cousin or aunt—her clothes billow when she runs, or wrap around her legs. Colourful. She seems to like colourful clothes and pays no attention to coordinating colours. Sometimes she wears layers of dresses of all different lengths, even when it's warm. The colours of the layers clash—like yesterday she wore a tank top that was pumpkin orange, a long under-skirt that was deep blue and a shorter over-skirt that was ...mauve. Summer Lilac, in fact. Approximate age: 7 years old. But skinny as a ...

It's hard to describe people even though, as a writer, I have to do it all the time. Sometimes it's not how people look at all that makes them so easy to recognize. Like the girl from next door. I know I wrote all about her baggy dresses in my notebook, but it's actually the way she moves, like a whirlwind, that makes her so distinctive. She never walks anywhere.

I'm spying on her right now, in fact. I found another tree to work in right down by the end of our driveway. From here I can see along the neighbour's driveway to the place where it curves away towards their house. Unfortunately, I can't see the neighbours' house, but I can see the girl. As usual, she's running. Back and forth along the driveway. She keeps stopping and looking at something in her hand. Then she jots quick notes in a book. That's what I mean about how I don't need to be up close or see the colour of her eyes to know what she's like.

I know she loves to run, that she is pretty "girly" (all those dresses and her hair is long), and that she is poor (those raggedy dresses actually give me lots of clues about her). I don't think she has any brothers or sisters because every time I see her she's alone.

"Alyssum?"

A man's voice yells from around the bend of the driveway. The girl stops, checks her wristwatch and then yells back, "I'm over here!"

The man shouts something else but I can't hear what it is because right then a dog starts barking. "Take Sandy!"

A golden retriever gallops towards the girl, wriggling and squirming and bouncing up and down. Alyssum turns and runs down the driveway, her arms pumping vigorously, her reddish-brown hair streaming out behind her. Our driveways are pretty close together so I can see how red her face is when she reaches the side of the road and sticks her hand into her mailbox. It's shaped like a birdhouse. Ours is just a plain old grey mailbox that squeaks when you open the door.

Of course, there's nothing inside. I know because that's why I'm down at the end of the driveway in the first place. I'm waiting for the mail truck to come by. I'm hoping that I'll get a letter from the *Millennium Review Quarterly* telling me that they accepted my kitchen poem for publication. After Marion Alsworthy told me I had real promise, I worked a lot on that poem. So far, four poetry magazines have written to me to say they don't want it.

My dad says that all artists must suffer and rejection is one of the best punishments for poets. Sometimes it's hard to tell when my dad is joking. Sometimes I think he brought me here to this dumb island to make sure I have an unhappy childhood so I have lots of stuff to write about.

The problem is, it's hard to imagine making a good story out of sitting in a tree waiting for the mail truck to come. Maybe when I run away a dangerous escaped criminal will see me sitting in the bus terminal and he'll decide that I would be a great accomplice for a fraud scheme. He'd dress me up to look innocent and sweet and then I'd stop people in the street, tell them I'm lost, and ask them for a little money for the bus. Then I'd have to hand all the money over to him because he would have a gun and I would have to sleep in a cardboard box under a bridge. I'd learn to drink Scotch whisky and swallow my pride to eat the leftover pizza crusts people throw into the garbage.

It would be a tough life, horrible—I'd cry myself to sleep every night and then a kind street worker would find me and maybe even adopt me. And that street worker would make sure I had decent notebooks and even though my life would have been dreadfully intense, I'd have lots to write about. I could probably win prizes for work like that.

Alyssum is looking up and down the road. I take pity on her. She's probably waiting for the family welfare cheque to arrive.

"Hi!"

She turns her head in my general direction and looks even more confused. I forget that I can see her but she can't see me.

"In the tree!"

She spots me and gives me a little wave. Mia hurtles out of the bushes and throws herself at the girl's golden retriever.

"Mia!" I scramble out of the tree and run over to rescue the other dog from my killer animal. Mia may only be a quarter the size of Sandy, but she's doing her best to smother the neighbours' dog with quick licks. We grab our dogs and say hello.

"The mail lady hasn't come yet," I offer.

"Is your mom really a vet?"

Up close I can see her eyes are a greeny-grey colour. They are open very wide and all around the middle little flecks of gold make them sparkle. Details like that are very important. I hope we don't talk too long so I can remember to write them down.

"Yes. Dr. Blake, DVM—that's my mom."

People don't know how annoying it is to talk about Mom's job. They always think being a vet is interesting.

"I want to be a vet when I grow up."

"Vet college is very expensive," I say. "It takes a long time."

I can't see any reason to build up Alyssum's hopes. My parents often grumble and complain about how much university educations cost these days. Somebody like Alyssum from a poor family doesn't have much hope of paying for a proper education.

"This is Sandy. Once I took a piece of glass out of her foot with my tweezers. My dad held her for me. She was very squirmy."

I can just imagine. Sandy is a very squirmy dog. Alyssum's trying hard to hold her back, but Sandy keeps bumping my hip with her head until I finally reach down to pat her. Then her whole body starts twisting and waggling with doggy pleasure. Mia, who's tucked under my other arm, nearly goes berserk with jealousy and Alyssum giggles.

"Hello, girls!"

I turn around and am shocked to realize I'm having another hallucination. For a minute, I think the woman driving the mail truck is Mrs. McAuley, my grade three teacher from my old school.

"Hi, Penny." Alyssum runs to the woman and takes two stacks of letters before Penny, the mail lady, even has a chance to reach out of her sliding door and jam them in the mailboxes.

"Penny makes the best chamomile tea—with chamomile from her garden," Alyssum says as the truck pulls away. "She sweetens it with honey from her own hives. Here, these are yours."

There's nothing from the *Millennium Review Quarterly* in the stack of letters. Nothing from Granny and Grandpa, either, and not even a postcard from Maggie. What a waste of time, waiting for the mail. I've already written four letters to Maggie, two to Granny and Grandpa, and one each to my other friends, Racquel and Anna. I guess it's time to write one to Charlie. Maybe he'll write back to me.

I try to see where Alyssum's letters are from without being too obvious about it. All I can identify is some kind of gardening magazine and a bunch of plain brown envelopes that look that bills. At least, they look like the envelopes with windows that always make my parents groan. That figures. Alyssum's parents are probably behind with paying their bills.

Alyssum flips quickly through her stack of letters and smiles when she comes to a letter from UNICEF.

"I've been waiting for this," she says.

Now *this* is interesting—I didn't know that UNICEF helped poor kids in Canada. I guess that the envelope has money in it, but I know it would be rude to come right out and ask how much, so I don't.

"Do you want to play sometime?" Alyssum asks.

"Sure. Sometime."

I wish I could go with her right away, to see her house. I wonder if she has her own bed or if she has to sleep with her whole family in one big bed.

"But not right now. I've gotta go. My mom's waiting for the mail," I say.

She shrugs and spins around, her skirts lifting away from her legs, and then races away down her driveway. Sandy gallumphs along beside her, barking snuffled little woofs every few steps.

Mia twists up, licks my neck, and whines. For a small dog she sure gets heavy fast. I put her down and we jog back to the house to give Mom the mail and then I head to the altar to make some notes in my journal.

Alyssum. Tragically sad girl from next door. No friends. No money. No taste in clothes. She seems desperate for a friend. Maybe not too bright. She may be older than I first thought. Eight. Maybe nine. Nine and scrawny. Poor thing. I don't think I like her. I can't imagine that we have anything in common.

Chapter Five

Collected Quote #4
Writing is a dog's life, but the only one worth living.—
Gustave Flaubert
Source: Charlie at the Old VB

Dear Charlie,

How are you? I am fine. Well, not really. We are more or less settled into the farm now. The builders have finally finished making the last changes to the house. Mom is really busy already. It didn't take long for her to get customers! She was worried about that before we came, but I guess she didn't have to be.

I suppose the farm is kind of pretty—we have four apple trees, three pear trees, a plum tree, and some kind of nut tree. Did you know nuts grow on trees? For some reason I thought they grew on bushes, or under the ground, but Mom says that's just peanuts and we don't have the right kind of weather or soil here to grow peanuts. That's too bad because then we could have made our own peanut butter.

If you are thinking this farm is like my grandparents' farm (remember I told you about it?), you are wrong. This place has rolling hills all around, some parts that are open fields, and some very big old trees in our very own forest that's about the size of the little park near your shop. I found a place that would be perfect for a tree-house. If I was into building treehouses, that is.

We also have a big space for a vegetable garden, one big old barn, one small old barn, a couple of sheds and other stuff. Dad told me this place was once owned by pirates, but I think he was kidding. Maybe I'll dig around a bit. Who knows, maybe I'll find some treasure and then I'd be rich and could come and visit you. I might do that anyway, visit I mean.

There is one part of our farm that I like a lot. We have a little stream at the very bottom end of the property. It flows through this place with some very tall trees that have pale green moss hanging from their branches. I like it because it reminds me of that place in Narnia where Lucy meets Mr. Tumnus—except of course there's no snow. I bet that during the winter, if we get any snow (the mail lady says most years it doesn't snow at all here) it would really look like Narnia.

I'm working a lot on my writing. If you see Marion Alsworthy in the store, could you please say hello from me? I don't want her to forget about me.

Please write back soon.

Your book-loving pal,
Heather

I bug Mom until she agrees to take me into town to mail the letter. It's only after I drop the envelope in the box that I remember Charlie always closes the shop in August and goes away to Newfoundland for the rest of the summer. So, now there's another person who won't write to me.

It turns out Dad also has some stuff to do in town and Matt always likes a trip to Rosehip, so while we're waiting to meet up after going to the post office, I manage to convince Mom to take me to look at notebooks.

"What's wrong with this one?"

"Boring."

"Heather, what does it matter?"

It is impossible to explain to my mother how

important it is to have a proper notebook. Ever since the tongue episode, I've been trying not to get into too many arguments with her. The office supply store in Rosehip is really just a corner of the drugstore which also has a grocery section and a stand for locally grown vegetables out front on the sidewalk. Because it's so small, the only notebooks they have are the kind with plain covers, the ones you are supposed to use in school.

Back in Toronto, there were about five thousand excellent stationery shops. The best one was called Pandora's Paper Box. Pandora's had notebooks with beautiful handmade paper and covers with flowers pressed into them, journals with locks and fine ribbons to mark the last page, huge hardbound books with plain pages that were great for doing drawings to go along with stories, and even some imported from Japan that had the most gorgeous, soft rice paper that just begged for poetry or deep secrets. If I had known how hard it would be to find a decent notebook on Tarragon Island, I would have stocked up and brought a box full with me.

"Why do you need another notebook?"

Sometimes my mother is so clueless it makes me think I was switched at birth. But, that's not likely since everybody says we look a lot like each other. Even I notice it now that I'm nearly as tall as she is.

Mom is a bit rounder than I am but she has the same dark eyes and dark hair (though I see her in front of the bathroom mirror in the mornings searching for silver hairs—she wraps them around her finger and yanks them out). I'm not going to do that. When I get grey hairs I'm going to leave them alone because I think grey hair makes you look wise. Besides, it must hurt to pull out your hair.

"Heather? Don't ignore me, please. Why do you

need another notebook?"

"I've nearly finished my old one and I'm thinking of starting a new novel so really I need two so I can keep all my notes and stuff in one place."

"A new novel? What happened to the one about the angels?"

It's really obvious from the way the sales girl is standing pretending to reorganize the business card samples on the counter that she is listening to our conversation.

"I'm still working on that one. But now I've started a new one, too. About poverty and despair."

I hope this will satisfy my mother, but she keeps right on going with her questions.

"Why can't you finish the angel book first—and, by the way, I hope you decide to give it a happy ending because people hate to read about children dying—and *then* you could start the next project. Poverty and despair?" A worried look flickers across her face but disappears when she checks her watch and sighs.

I want to say that she should appreciate the fact I don't try to tell her how to neuter dogs, but I can tell she just wants to get out of the store and spend the least amount of money possible without looking cheap. Judging by the impatient way she is fiddling with her handbag, if I'm not careful I'm not going to get any notebook at all. When a writer is desperate, plain and ugly is better than nothing.

"Mom, please—I'll pay you back. I'll do some extra chores." I know she also wants to get back to the clinic to check on the orphaned squirrel she's bottle feeding, and that she promised to go up to the other end of the island to look at someone's sick scarlet macaw. It seems to me she's busier here than she was in Toronto, though she keeps saying how she likes the slower pace of island life.

At the till, the girl (whose name tag reads "Sunny" and who seems to be laughing at some kind of private joke) says, "Have you seen the paper lady at the market?"

I shake my head. Saturday mornings are always busy at the clinic, so we haven't been to the island's weekly market yet. We've certainly heard lots about it, though, and it sounds like just about the most interesting thing that happens on this rock.

"Tonya Windwoman. She creates her own paper and binds it into the most beautiful books—journals and stuff. Maybe that would be more what you're looking for?"

"This will be fine for now," my mom says, though I would have liked to find out more about the paper lady.

"Come on, Heather. We have to find your father and brother. I think they were trying to get Dad's bike tire fixed."

In the car on the way home, Mom won't stop talking about the "lifestyle incident" at the store.

"Ben, it was just such a great example of how people here think differently than they do in the big city. There I was, standing at the till with my money out, and this girl was saying we should go to the market because she didn't have any notebooks like Heather wanted. Obviously, I just bought the notebooks anyway because, really, a notebook is a notebook is a notebook, right?"

Obviously, I don't say anything from the back seat because I don't feel like starting a fight. My dad jumps right in with a story of his own.

"I took my bike to the garage to get them to look at the flat tire—and you know, they patched it and blew it up and didn't charge me a dime! That would never have happened in Toronto!"

I never knew my parents were such cheapskates. Since we moved here, they are always commenting on how generous people are and how nobody is chasing the almighty dollar. I don't know. They forget about people like Charlie who used to give me books of poetry for my collection, especially if the corners were a bit bent or he had lots of copies of something.

It's like, now that they've moved their whole family across the country, they have to make it seem like every little thing that happens proves it was a good idea. Which, of course, it wasn't. I don't care what the rest of my family does: I'm still going *home*. How could anybody honestly want to live in a place where there's no bus to town, where there are no good people to be friends with, and where there isn't even a skateboard park? Not that I like skate-boarding—I don't—but if I did, I'd have a hard time coping with the gravel roads and lack of sidewalks.

Unfortunately, saving up for a bus ticket isn't going very well. Now that I owe Mom for the notebooks (she broke down and bought me two), I'm actually in the hole and I can't imagine how many hours of chores it will take before I have enough saved up to get out of here.

"Where's Dad?"

"On the boat."

That figures. I've had the paint for my writer's cottage for four days, but the chicken coop still looks like a chicken coop and Dad is always playing with that boat. He's barely spending any time at all painting in his studio.

Matt and I are cleaning out the dog runs, my least favourite job in the world. The people who owned the place before us bred champion cocker spaniels. When Mom and Dad were looking at possible places to buy, Mom got all excited about the kennels and decided she could use them for boarding dogs when their families went away on holidays. Since it was her idea, I think she should be the one to clean out the kennels every day.

"Stop playing with that dog!"

Matt's only nine but that's no excuse to play with the boarders instead of hosing out the runs.

"This is *work*. I'm playing with Chartreuse because her owner said she won't eat unless she's happy. It would be cruel to ignore her."

Chartreuse is a mop on short legs, some kind of lapdog with a stupid name. "Chartreuse" is a colour—a pale yellowy green. It doesn't even make sense to name a dog after a colour like that. Matt is in her run sitting cross-legged on the concrete. The dog is sitting in his lap, leaning against his chest, her chin tucked up under his. He is slowly stroking underneath her tummy. Chartreuse has her eyes closed and every few strokes gives a little sigh and snuggles closer.

Mia is a different kind of small dog. Dad says she's got the soul of a wolf trapped in a vertically challenged body. Chartreuse, on the other hand, has the soul of a marshmallow.

I blast the empty run where I'm working, swoosh the jet of water back and forth over the ground, chase the bits of dirt down the drain. I'm tempted to turn the hose on Matt but that silly little dog would probably get traumatized and then I'd be in real trouble.

I wish Dad would forget about his dumb boat and get to work on the cottage. I'm getting pretty desperate for a private place to work. It's not too comfortable sitting up in trees and I don't like my room. It's small and hot and I don't like the way the furniture is organized. I don't like being in the house, either, because at any time somebody can just come and knock on my door or, in the case of Matt, come barging in without warning.

"Heather? Matt?" Dad walks toward us, still

wearing the shorts and canvas hat he always wears when he's in boat mode.

I shut off the nozzle and the hiss of water stops.

"Hi, Dad. Can we work on my cottage this afternoon?"

"Maybe later, after we get back."

"Where are we going?" Matt asks, still sitting on the ground with Chartreuse.

"Sailing!" Dad beams as if Christmas has come early.

Matt kisses Chartreuse on the top of her head and jumps up. "Is Mom coming, too?"

Dumb question. Mom is working. Mom is always working. In fact, today she is working in two places at the same time. About an hour ago, some sheep farmer from down the road came roaring into the driveway in a truck that had two painted rainbows arching over the hood. All that colour didn't do much to disguise the fact the truck was about a thousand years old.

The farmer was all out of breath and told Mom that one of his lambs had got caught in a barbed wire fence. Mom rushed off, leaving Milly at the front desk to tell people with regular appointments about the emergency.

Sailing isn't something Mom can easily fit into her schedule. That's something else people don't understand about vets. Animals don't plan their accidents at convenient times. Sometimes Mom even has to get up in the middle of the night if a dog or cat gets hit by a car.

That's another thing that's different about living on Tarragon Island—the kind of animals Mom has to help. Last week I heard the phone ring at two in the morning. When I asked Mom about it the next day, she told us that a deer had been hit and she had to go and help. There weren't any deer in Toronto, though sometimes Mom had to deal with raccoons. Anyway, the deer was already dead by the time Mom arrived on the scene, so there wasn't anything she could do.

I wanted to know about the driver of the car. That kind of terrible event can be a life-changing experience and life-changing experiences can make good stories. But in this case, even though the little car was pretty smashed up, the driver was fine. Mom would never make a good witness at a crime scene or a good writer for that matter, since she couldn't remember what colour the car was, if it had four doors or two, nothing. I asked her about the driver, hoping she could provide me with some interesting information.

"She was about my age, nearly forty, with long hair tied back in a pony tail."

"Why was she on the road at two in the morning?"

"Heather, I didn't ask her. We all just wanted to go home to bed."

Another reason my mother would be a lousy writer is that she's not nearly nosy enough. Because she couldn't tell me anything intriguing, I had to make the rest up. I wrote in my journal:

Beatrice Cinnamon Butter (everyone on this island is named after some kind of food or season or plant) was driving home from a party at her sister's house, singing about ... singing a love song to her new boyfriend, Strong Oak ... except the woman in the car had been alone in real life. Not a problem, not a problem, Heather. Think. Strong Oak was already married to somebody else, so when the deer jumped out in front of the car and Beatrice Cinnamon Butter hit the brakes sighing, "Oh my, we are doomed!" Strong Oak jumped out of the passenger's seat and ran and hid in the bushes until after the police and the vet had come and gone.

Dumb story, I know. But sometimes I have to think of ten stupid story ideas before I come up with a good one.

"Right, Heather?"

"Sorry, what?"

Dad repeats slowly, "You can help Matt with his reading while we're on the boat."

That explains why Matt suddenly doesn't look so thrilled about going sailing. I know better than to open my mouth. I've had way too many lectures already about how important it is to "be supportive." Matt can't read. Well, that's a bit of an exaggeration. He can sort of read—but very slowly and it's hard for him because he has dyslexia. He can't write, either. He turns some of his letters backwards and upside down so when he wants to write a small letter *b* it might come out like a small letter *p* or sometimes *q* or sometimes a *d*. It's very confusing. I'm pretty good at figuring out his notes, but it's hard not to tease him when he writes "pleze dring em som bodsicles" instead of "please bring me some popsicles."

The advantage to his bad writing is that Mom says she will buy him just about anything if he at least tries to write a note. Last week I bribed him to write a note to Mom because I really wanted a new pen. Good pens are as important to a writer as just the right kind of journal. Matt wrote, "dleze duy my a qen." Mom said, "Did your sister put you up to this?" I guess a pen isn't something Matt would really want for himself, since he hates writing so much.

Matt is a lousy liar, but he tried. He said, "If I had just the right pen maybe I'd be inspired." He's not dumb—he just can't read and write.

Unfortunately, Mom didn't buy it and we both got in trouble—Matt for lying and me for bribery, using my younger brother for illegal gains, and something else. That's why we had to wash out the dog runs for no money, which is why I still haven't made any progress with my bus ticket fund.

"Can Heather read to me?"

Matt loves to hear stories. He has an amazing

memory and can quote whole passages even if he only hears them once.

"The deal is, you have to practise your own reading for the same amount of time Heather reads aloud." My dad is trying to sound calm and nurturing. When I write about my dad, I use words like that because I believe it captures the way he really is. Recently, though, I've started using words like "distracted," "distant," and "boat-obsessed" because recently he has been all those things.

I don't understand it. His sailboat is kind of a wreck. It stinks below decks and nothing on it seems to work right. There was a good reason he got it so cheap. Lots of good reasons, in fact. Ever since he bought it he has been trying to get it fixed up so we can all go on sailing adventures.

"It just wasn't possible for me to sail when I was a boy."

That's what he said to Mom when he was trying to convince her what a great idea it was to get a boat. Mom's reaction was really strange. She held his hand and said, so kindly, "It's completely up to you. What do you want to do?"

"I know I don't want to tell my mother!"

They both laughed like they realized how odd that sounded. It sure was strange to think a grown-up would care what his mother thought! I couldn't imagine why Nana would care if Dad had a sailboat.

"Whatever you decide is okay with me."

The weird part was that it didn't sound as though Mom was humouring him, like the time in Toronto when he decided to join the model airplane club. He set the garage on fire when he had an accident with some spilled gasoline. Then when she said, "Don't worry, dear, I'm sure you'll learn about ignitions if you keep going to the meetings," she was definitely saying it to make him feel better.

The way Mom looked at him when he talked about his deprived-of-sailing childhood was with real concern, more like the way she looked at Matt that time he fell off the top of the slide at the playground and hit his head.

"Maybe the dreams will stop if I get my own boat," I overheard Dad say the afternoon they decided to go ahead and make an offer on *Ariel*.

Neither Matt nor I dream about sailing. I wrote down what Dad said about dreaming in my journal because I once heard a psychologist on a radio phone-in show say that a lot of men of a certain age have the same dream (about going sailing) and this kind of information is just what I need for characters in my books. Not that I have any plans to write a story about a man of a certain age and his boat, because the whole idea of going sailing is very boring to me.

At the marina, when we load the picnic food, a big blanket, life jackets, and my backpack full of books for me and Matt, *Ariel* tips from side to side in the water. Dad holds my wrist when I climb aboard. I don't like the tippy feeling of the boat, but Matt doesn't even seem to notice. He finds a place near the back of the cockpit and perches on the seat, his knees pulled up under his chin, his brown eyes squinting into the sun.

Chapter Six

Collected Quote #43
The difference between the right word and nearly the right word is the same as that between lightning and the lightning bug.—Mark Twain
Source: <u>Writing: The Basics,</u> by Bert Chester

"Can we have a picnic on that island?"

The island Matt's pointing to is right in the harbour. It looks so close we could probably swim to it.

"I thought we'd head over to Billy's Cove." Dad pulls a long skinny map out of the cabin and unfolds it. "Have a look at the chart. We're here . . . this is Goat Head Island, the one we'll go right past as we leave the harbour. Over here on the chart, this is Billy's Cove on the east side of Billy's Island. It's too far away to see, but once we get clear of Goat Head, we turn left . . . north."

Our destination is about three chart folds away. "How long will it take?" I ask.

"We should be there in a couple of hours."

I calculate quickly. Two hours there, an hour for a picnic, two hours back. No way we're going to get to my writer's cottage today.

Dad pulls on the engine cord five or six times before he realizes he has forgotten to flip on the starting switch.

A cloud of blue-grey smoke putters from the back of the outboard. Dad turns the throttle and the boat begins to pull away from the dock.

"Ahhh!" Dad yells something about lines and I have no idea what he's talking about. Matt's eyes get very big and his mouth opens and shuts but I can't hear anything he's saying because of the engine which is suddenly very loud. Dad waves his hand wildly in the air and then I see that the ropes that had tied us to the dock are still tied to the dock!

Dad swats at the ignition switch and the engine stops, and *Ariel* stops straining at her tethers.

"Can I give you a hand?"

An old guy with a thick, red wool sweater strolls along the dock until he's even with Dad, who is fumbling around with the engine. "I, uhhh, the engine, uhhh, caught and revved and I wasn't quite ready. . . ."

The old guy's boots are level with my eyes. They're big, wide, yellow Wellington boots that look older than he is. One of the soles is fastened to the rest of the boot with grey duct tape that the old man has wrapped around the toe about fifty times. I think he must be a sailor because Dad said that every sailor worth his salt always has a good supply of duct tape on hand for emergency repairs.

"Throttle stuck?" the old sailor asks kindly.

"Yeah, yeah that's it," Dad agrees quickly.

With the duct tape man on the dock to handle the lines, it doesn't take long for Dad to fire up the engine again and we slip away from the dock and into the quiet water of the harbour.

My science teacher last year said that glass is actually a very, very thick kind of liquid which is why in old buildings, the panes are thicker at the bottom than at the top. I can't imagine anything "dripping" down that slowly but he brought in an old pane of glass to show us and it really was thicker at the bottom.

I'm thinking of glass because the water is so still it looks like thick, green glass. I crawl forward on *Ariel's* deck and lie on my tummy right at the very front. I hang my head over the edge and stare down. The point of the prow slices the water, carving it into two ridges that rise above the water's surface and peel away behind us, fanning out in a wide *V*. Up front, I can hardly hear the engine and as I stare at the splitting water it feels like I'm being hypnotized.

I try to relax my eyes because I'm starting to feel a little dizzy looking down into the water, and suddenly I'm in the middle of a dream I'd totally forgotten.

In the dream, Grandpa is sitting on top of the fridge in his house and a big wind is blowing through the kitchen.

"What's this?" I ask, holding up a fork the size of a rake. When I move the giant fork around, trails of sparkles flow out of the ends of the tines. The sparks are just like birthday sparklers, cool and prickly and a little scary. Grandpa doesn't answer my question.

"Climb aboard," he says.

Then I'm floating on the stream of sparks and whirling around the kitchen and I'm getting very excited, like I'm about to go on a journey. I float past Grandpa who is now lying curled up on the fridge like a huge cat. He smiles at me and nods towards the open window.

I want to see where I'll go on the trail of sparks, but right then Matt plunks down beside me and pokes me in the ribs with his foot.

"Can you read to me now?"

I open the book, *Charlie and the Chocolate Factory*, and start reading. We're at the part where Augustus

Gloop, the greedy kid on the chocolate factory tour, falls into the river of melted chocolate.

After I've read about three chapters, I suggest that Matt take a turn.

"I don't feel like it. You keep reading."

"You promised Dad you'd read the same amount as—"

"I'll read all the way back. That would be fair."

I look back at Dad who is all by himself in the cockpit.

"When are we going to put up the sails?" I yell.

Dad shrugs and holds up his hands. "No wind!"

It's true. Even though we're out in the strait and away from the sheltered harbour, the water is calm. The only ripples are caused by us puttering along. It's more like we're on a lake than the ocean. Since I don't have to help with the sails I nearly finish the whole book as we motor all the way to Billy's Cove. The cove is a sheltered bay that doesn't look a whole lot different from our harbour back on Tarragon Island, except there are no houses, no road, and no marina.

It takes forever to fiddle around with the anchor to make sure it's set properly. By the time Dad is satisfied we aren't going to drift onto any sharp rocks, we're all ravenous.

"You know, I don't think we have time to go ashore for the picnic," he says, looking at his watch.

"What!?" Matt pulls a terrible face. If *I* had done that, I would have been in big trouble. "Where are we going to eat?"

We don't have a lot of choices.

"The foredeck?" I offer.

"Sounds good to me. Matt, be a sport. Next time we'll leave earlier and then we can go ashore and explore. But it's not sensible to leave for home too late. It wouldn't be safe to travel after dark since we don't know these waters very well."

There's no point in arguing. I spread out the old grey blanket on the foredeck and we lay out the food. It's not a bad picnic, considering we didn't have a lot of planning time. There are buns, cookies, juice, cheese, tomatoes, and potato chips.

"I'm so hungry!" Matt says with his mouth full of a cheese and potato chip sandwich. It takes no time at all to devour just about everything we brought along. It strikes me how silly it was to motor all the way here just so we could sit on the deck to have lunch. We could have done that back at the marina and then we still would have had time to work on my writer's cottage.

So, after our quick visit to the island we only get to look at from a distance, we pull up the anchor and Dad tries to start up the engine. It sputters and coughs and dies three times in a row and that's when Dad discovers we barely have enough gas left to make it to the end of the cove, never mind all the way home again.

"Damn."

Dad's staring at the empty gas tank as if by looking at it harder he can magically fill it up. He bangs around in the lockers under the seats in the cockpit, looking for spare gas. Then, since we're drifting closer to shore, he quickly throws the anchor overboard again. It hisses down into the murky green water trailing a whoosh of tiny bubbles.

"Dad, how will we get home?" Matt's voice shakes a little.

I laugh. "Hey, Mattie, look at it this way. If we're stuck here for days, there's more time for me to read to you!"

Matt scowls. I turn to Dad and ask, "What about the radio?"

Dad shoots me a look that says, "Don't you think

I would have radioed for help by now if I could have?" I know I should keep my mouth shut, but Matt's nervousness is contagious.

"You mean, we don't have a radio?"

"Of course we have a radio."

"So, what's the problem?"

"It doesn't work."

"So you mean we have to wait here until . . . what, the wind comes up? That could be weeks."

"What are we going to eat?" Matt's eyes are getting rounder by the minute. He has a good point. We ate most of the food we brought for our picnic lunch. There isn't even a house around the edge of the cove where we could go to call for help. *Ariel* is the only boat anchored here.

"The human body can last eighty-three days without food. As long as we have water we'll be okay," Dad says reassuringly. I'm suddenly so thirsty I can't think of anything else.

"I'm thirsty," Matt says.

"You two are not being very helpful. Go below and see what supplies we have on board. The leftovers won't go far."

A twenty-four-foot sailboat is not very big, so I'm not sure where Dad figures we're going to find a hidden cache of food. But there's nothing to lose, so we crawl into the V-berth in the front, pointy part of the boat, and lift up the cushions to get at the storage lockers underneath. We find a spare anchor, coils of rope and chain, some mouldy flares, and a couple of empty water jugs, but nothing to eat.

In the tiny head, there's nothing but the low pump toilet, and even that doesn't seem to work quite right. The narrow galley has a table that folds down into a bed and a narrow berth opposite that. Underneath all the seats are more storage spaces.

Matt and I search through all the drawers, cabinets, boxes, and bags looking for food. We carry everything we find that looks remotely edible up to Dad, who has spread out the chart on top of the cabin.

"One full bottle of orange pop. Two granola bars. Two oranges. One crusty bun. A quarter of a package of cookies. And *my* water bottle." I put each item on one of the cockpit seats along with two rolls of duct tape. It isn't much of a spread, though if we have to repair something, we're in good shape.

"*Your* water bottle?" Matt snatches it.

"Give that back!"

"This is an emergency. You have to share!"

"You should have planned better! I never leave home without my water bottle!"

"I don't like orange pop!" Matt's face is all red and his eyes look slightly crazed.

"Kids! Stop! It's not like we're a thousand miles from civilization. When we don't show up tonight, your mother might just notice."

"We have to stay here all night? How will she know where to find us? Did you tell her where we were going?" For every question I ask I can think of three more things I want to know.

For the tenth time in about as many minutes, Dad looks sheepish. "I didn't actually decide where we were going until we got to the boat," he admits.

We all slump onto the seat opposite the food. It's a pathetic sight. I wonder who's going to get the crusty bun for supper.

"I think we should *do* something," Matt says, trying not to cry.

"That's what I was thinking," Dad says, nodding wisely. "Here on the chart it looks like there's a radio tower over on the other side of Billy's Island. Maybe there's a building of some kind there, too."

"I wonder who Billy was?"

"Who cares, Heather." Matt leans over the map and peers at the place where Dad is pointing. We all know it's kind of useless, since if there's anything Matt reads worse than words it's maps, but Matt looks anyway.

"*I* care about Billy. Maybe he was a pirate or something and I could use him in a story."

"Nobody wants to read your stupid stories."

I give Matt a shove. He was there this morning when the letter came from the *Millennium Review Quarterly*. The photocopied note said, "Sorry, we are not able to publish your submission at this time."

"At least *I* can write!"

"Heather!" My dad is furious.

"Sorry. Sorry, Matt." And I *am* sorry because I know how hard it is for him to read and write and I know it's really, really mean to tease him. But he should know how mean it is to tease me about never getting published anywhere.

It's too late, though. Matt is crying. "Matt, I'm really, truly sorry. I didn't mean it."

"Leave me alone!" He scrubs at his cheeks with the back of his hand. "I don't care. I just want to go home."

"Hey, Matt—we'll be home soon. Let's think of this as a great adventure." Dad has his arm around Matt's shoulders and he is giving me one of his "you've really gone too far this time" looks.

"Matt—you said we should do something and you're right," I say, trying desperately to think of a way to make Matt feel better. "What about taking the dinghy over to the island? Since we can't rush off anywhere now, we could explore and see if someone has a cabin . . . or maybe over on the other side there's a pay phone."

"A pay phone?" Dad and Matt say in unison. Matt grins—he can't help it. "That's the dumbest idea," he says. But I can tell he's feeling a little better.

"Someone should stay with the boat," Dad says, "to make sure we're not dragging that anchor. Do you think you two could manage to row to shore?"

He doesn't sound at all convinced this is a good idea even though the shore is not very far away. We can see all the rocks and logs on the beach.

"Row? I could swim," Matt says bravely.

"Not in this water. You'd freeze before you got halfway there!" There's a note of real alarm in Dad's voice and it seems like maybe he won't let us go after all.

"I'm just kidding, Dad."

We all sigh at the same time. It's terrible when we get all stressed out and can't even tell when someone is joking.

"Let's go," I say, grabbing my water bottle and tossing it into the dinghy we've towed along behind us all day. Sometimes instead of having a long discussion about something, it's better to just jump right in and do it.

Matt doesn't need any encouragement. He scrambles down into the rowboat after me before Dad changes his mind.

"Be careful," Dad says, leaning down and steadying the dinghy. It sounds like he's more scared than he wants to admit.

"We will!" we say, and then I slip the oars into the locks and slowly start to row away.

Reluctantly, Dad lets go of the painter and Matt pulls in the end of the rope so we don't drag it through the water.

It doesn't take us long at all to get to the beach. The little wooden dinghy crunches against the rocks and shells in the shallow water.

"Careful! You'll get a hole in the bottom!" Matt sounds really worried.

"Jump out!" He splashes into the water and steadies the boat while I climb out. My sneakers immediately fill with icy water. Yuck.

We pull the dinghy up onto the shore and tie it to a big driftwood log.

"Will it be safe, do you think?"

"Matt, there's nobody around for miles. Who do you think is going to steal it?"

But inside, I'm thinking exactly what he's thinking. I know the chart says the island is uninhabited, but it still feels creepy to be walking around on land. When we start picking our way along the shoreline, I keep looking over my shoulder to see if anyone is following us.

In Toronto, we couldn't go anywhere alone and here we are roaming around a strange place totally unsupervised. It's spooky and exciting at the same time.

Chapter Seven

July 25. Aboard Ariel. Midnight, sitting up on the foredeck with a flashlight.

A 24 foot boat is not big enough for three people and a wild Canada goose! This is what happened. Matt and I went to Billy's Island to try to find help, or at least water. It was very hard to walk along the beach because of all the prickly barnacles and pointy rocks that were covered with a kind of green slime. Matt slipped and he cut his hand on a rock. A razor sharp rock. A razor sharp rock that was waiting like a ... like a—come on, Heather, description, description—like an ant lion waiting for an ant to fall unsuspectingly into its lair.

Well, anyway, Matt slipped and cut his hand on a rock. He was crying so I said we should try and get away from the beach for a while to see if there was an easier way to walk to get to the other side of the island. He wouldn't stop crying and I was thinking we should have brought matches and string so we could build a fire and a shelter. But of course our "adventure" isn't going like you read about in books or I wouldn't be so hungry right now.

So, we were sitting on this big log way up at the edge of the forest and I was telling Matt my idea for the novel about poverty and despair when he suddenly grabbed my arm and totally forgot about his cut.

"What's that?" he said with alarm bells going off in his voice.

"A piece of plastic," I said maturely and calmly.

"No way," he said insistently.

"What else could it be?" I asked persistently.

"I think it's a seal," he said more persistently.

"No way," I said determinedly.

It's too hard to write down whole conversations, so I'll just write down what happened next. We went over to the big flapping thing on the beach and when we got closer we could see it was a Canada goose that was all tangled up in some fishing net that was stuck under a big log. Part of the net was under the log, I mean, so the bird couldn't get away.

Matt said we couldn't leave the bird there because it would starve. And I said there was no way I was going near it because it had a huge beak and I thought it would bite me.

"It has a broken wing!" Matt said with worry crackling through his young but brave voice.

Matt went to the bird that was flapping around and trying to escape. He threw his jacket over the goose and then threw himself on top of the bird. A heroic struggle unfolded before my eyes, right there on the beach. Matt yelled at me to help but I didn't want to get closer because the goose's head and neck were still free and they were hissing around like a big black snake with beady eyes. Then the bird pecked Matt's arm and I jumped forward to protect my young and vulnerable brother.

"Put your sweatshirt on his head!" Matt yelled forcefully.

He didn't need to say anything because I'm sure I

would have thought of doing that myself. Anyway, I took off my sweatshirt and tossed it towards the bird and it mostly missed and Matt was the one who got the bird's head covered in the end.

I have to go because Dad says it's very late. Which is true. I'll finish this in the morning.

Since the goose is sleeping in the forepeak, there's not really enough room for all of us. We put the forepeak cushions on the cabin sole and that's where Dad sleeps, between and below me and Matt. We fold down the table and sleep on the two berths in the main cabin. Of course, we don't have enough blankets and no pillows at all so we have to make do with rain gear and life jackets. Matt gets the grey picnic blanket. I don't think that's fair at all but Dad said Matt's the smallest and most likely to get cold.

I don't think I'll ever fall asleep, but then I jerk awake when I hear a loud thump and Dad's voice saying, "Adam? Adam, are you there?"

"Dad?"

He doesn't answer for a minute and in the dim light I see his head poke up from the floor where he's sleeping.

"Sorry, Heather. I was dreaming."

He still sounds confused.

"Dad, are you okay?"

"I'm fine. Sorry. Go back to sleep."

"Who's Adam?"

"Adam?" Dad sounds kind of shocked, almost like I caught him saying a swear word. He lies back down and says, "Never mind. It was just a dream."

July 26—Dawn

I never get up at dawn, but I couldn't sleep because that Canada goose woke up early and was bashing around in the forepeak. Somehow he got free from our

55

sweatshirts. Matt and I kind of wrapped him up because Matt said we had to try to stop the goose from beating his injured wing around. But I think the goose got hot.

I thought of lots more stuff about the goose rescue I didn't have time to write yesterday. The hardest part was cutting through the fishing net with a sharp rock to get him free. Matt even had to bite through a bit of the net and he said it tasted like gasoline.

Anyway, Matt sat down in the bottom of the dinghy holding onto the goose who was pretty quiet as long as Matt kept his head covered. I rowed back and Dad was kind of mad except he knew we couldn't have left the bird there on the beach to die so he let us barricade the goose into the forepeak. I just checked on the goose and he knocked over the dish we put out last night with the last of the water from my water bottle in it. I hope he got a drink before he did that because we only have a bit of orange pop left and that's probably not very good for a goose.

"His wing is broken for sure. See how it hangs down like that?"

Dad and Matt are down below staring at the bird. I'm up in the cockpit staring at the horizon like people do when they are waiting to be rescued. When I first woke up, I thought about Dad's dream and wondered about this Adam guy. But then I got pretty distracted by the idea we might never get rescued and then I started thinking about more important things, like whether I should make a will.

Way off in the distance, past several islands, I can see the smokestack of a big ferry boat disappearing towards Vancouver. We are way too far away for anyone to see us waving.

"Do we have a mirror?" I ask suddenly.

"You mean to signal with?" Dad asks. "Good idea."

I hear him thudding around in the head and then the sound of breaking glass. "Damn."

He hands me a pretty big piece of mirror. "Be careful. It's sharp."

Sometimes grown-ups say the silliest things. What else would you expect when someone hands you a piece of broken mirror? I tilt it back and forth and the reflection of the sun blazes back towards the shore.

"That works well. But shine it over there. . . ."

I point it to one of the more distant islands, one where we can just see tiny houses. I tilt and flash for about fifteen minutes and then give up. For the third time this morning, I go below and search through the cupboards again looking for more food. We finished the rest of the cookies for breakfast and I'm still starving. I can't imagine how hungry the goose must be.

"I hope Mom can fix him," Matt says. "He's so beautiful."

Matt hadn't even eaten all his breakfast. He'd broken off some of his cookie to share with the bird. I felt guilty when he did that, but it was too late. I'd already finished my food.

Suddenly, the boat starts bobbing up and down as if Dad's jumping around on deck. We hear him yell at the top of his lungs.

"Hey! Heeeeeelp!"

Matt and I jostle each other out of the way as we both try to be the first up into the cockpit. A big, grey coast guard boat is heading straight towards us.

"Heeeeelp!" I shriek.

"Over here!!!" Matt yells.

"Shhhhh," my dad says. "They've seen us already." But then, he gets so excited he starts yelling again himself. "Helloooo! Help!"

"Ben Blake?" one of the men on the deck of the

coast guard boat calls through a megaphone.

"Yes!! Thank goodness you are here!"

Everything moves very quickly. One of the men jumps down into our boat and finds out what happened. He calls to somebody else to bring a can of gas and then there are three men plus Dad all in the cockpit fussing around with the gas and the engine.

Then Dad pulls the rope and the engine starts right up and the men all shake hands and smile and look important. One of the men scolds Dad about not having a working radio on board.

"But, I suppose you've learned your lesson?"

Dad nods and just like a little kid in trouble at school says, "We're going right home now, sir. Would you please let my wife know we're okay?"

"Already done, Mr. Blake."

The men board their big boat and we wave and they wave and we pull up the anchor and Dad turns *Ariel* around and we head back for Tarragon Island. The coast guard boat completely disappears.

It hits us all at about the same time.

"We didn't ask them for any food," Matt says, his bottom lip quivering.

"How much orange pop do we have left?" Dad asks.

Even though Matt doesn't like it very much, he takes a sip from the bottle when we pass it around. Then he goes back down below and spends the next two hours keeping an eye on the goose while I get back to work on my novel and concentrate on not being hungry.

Chapter Eight

Collected Quote #15
Writing is easy; all you have to do is sit staring at a blank sheet of paper until the drops of blood form on your forehead.—Gene Fowler
Source: Dad

"Ben! What happened?"

We're all hugging and excited and Mom is touching each of us in turn like she's checking to make sure we are real.

"Dad didn't get enough gas. . . ."

"Bobbi, honey, the radio didn't work—we have to get a new one. . . ."

"Mom, guess what? Matt saved a bird!"

We're all talking at once and everything is very confusing—so confusing that at first I don't even see the guy with the camera.

"This goose was stuck on the beach, in a net, and his wing is broken—can you fix him?" Matt's all out of breath.

"Goose?"

"Excuse me—my name is Allan Turnbull. Editor of the *Tarragon Times*."

"A Canada goose—he was stuck on the beach. . . ."

We're all pretty much ignoring Mr. Turnbull, who is the same size as me—in height, that is. He's about four times as round. He has a huge stomach, like he's pregnant. The rest of him, except maybe his cheeks which are also quite round with a splotch of red in the middle of each, is quite normal-looking. I'm not nervous at all when he introduces himself and says he wants to do a story about our rescue for the paper because I'm imagining what he would look like in bathing trunks.

I decide to describe him in detail in my journal because he looks just like the kind of man who would be the mayor of a middle-sized city and I could use a character like that in my novel about poverty and despair. He could be the one who rescues the tragically poor girl, Rosie, from her terrible life of rags and not enough food by being pleasant to her when they meet in an underground parking lot.

Thinking about food makes me feel queasy and weak. I grab onto Mom's arm and try to get her attention.

My dad notices and says, "Honey, we haven't eaten properly since lunch yesterday. I think we should all go to The Laughing Goblin for breakfast. The goose should be okay for a little longer if we fill his water dish. Would you like to join us, Mr. Turnbull?"

The five of us crowd around a small table at The Laughing Goblin—the only restaurant close to the marina where we keep *Ariel*. The three of us have sausages and pancakes and orange juice and milk and eat like we'd been marooned for twenty years, and not just overnight. When we finish (which doesn't take very long at all), Mr. Turnbull starts asking all kinds of questions. He is especially interested in the goose rescue.

"I have some notes I took about the goose," I offer. "Would you like to see them?"

"My sister's a writer," Matt pipes up.

"Really? Well then, would you like to write the article about your rescue? You were there, after all."

Mom and Dad look very proud. Dad pats Mom's hand on the table.

"Sure!" I say. Hemingway and lots of other novelists wrote stories for newspapers. This could be the true beginning of my career!

"Give me three hundred words. And, I need it by the end of the day tomorrow so it can run in this week's paper. I'll pay you five dollars."

I hope I don't look too stunned. *Pay?* I can't believe my luck. *Get paid to write?* It's totally unbelievable. While the grown-ups chat over coffee, I sit there, planning my story in my head.

"How's the story coming along?" Dad asks me that night at dinner.

We're all sitting outside on the deck munching on hot dogs and hamburgers from the barbecue. It's amazing how good everything tastes today. I had a grilled cheese sandwich for lunch and it was positively scrumptious. I wonder how long this will last?

"Fine," I say. I don't want to admit publicly that things are not going very well. So far, I've written the first sentence about a hundred times and it still sounds terrible.

"Why don't you read what you have so far," Mom says.

"Do you think there will be a photo of us with the story?" Matt asks.

"I don't have much so far."

"Let's hear it anyway."

I can tell they aren't going to leave me alone until I read something so I get my notebook and read. "Danger! Local boaters face starvation and isolation but survive."

The corners of Mom's mouth twitch. "Go on."

"That's all I've written."

Dad's eyebrow slides up. "But you've been working all afternoon."

"It's not that easy, you know. I mean, I have to grab the readers right from the first sentence."

"You don't have to lie," Matt says.

"I'm not lying. Don't tell me you weren't starving. And there weren't any other people around so we were isolated."

"Leave her alone," Mom says. "Heather, write the story the way you think it happened. Your editor will let you know if you have to change anything."

"If he's going to have time for changes, you'd better get it to him first thing in the morning," Dad says.

"May I be excused?"

Mom and Dad nod and I flee to the maple tree by the altar rock. I can just see the top of the chicken coop/writing cottage from my perch. It would sure be great if Dad and I could get it all fixed up since now that I am selling my articles, I need a proper place to work. If the paper buys my stuff regularly, maybe it won't take too long to save up for my trip. All the more reason to do a really excellent job. I know that papers like to have quotes from people, so I try to remember what we talked about on the boat.

"We should have checked the batteries in the radio," said Mr. Blake when he realized he had put his children's lives at risk.

I scratch out the sentence. It makes Dad sound too dumb.

"The most exciting part was when we found the goose," said nine-year-old Matt Blake.

Somehow that makes the dramatic goose rescue sound boring. Then I decide maybe I should turn it into a funny story.

I never thought I would wake up in the middle of a Gilligan's Island episode. Yesterday, when our ship set sail from an island port, the weather started getting rough. If not for the courage of her fearless crew, the Ariel would be lost.

Except the weather had been fine. Not a cloud in sight, in fact.

Before I know it, my posterior is getting numb because I've been sitting up in the tree for so long without moving and I still don't have a story.

"Mom?" I find her in the clinic doing paperwork. "I can't do this."

"Of course you can, Heather. You are a writer, remember?"

"How should I start it? Everything I try sounds stupid."

"Leave the beginning for now and just write the rest of the story. Maybe by the time you get to the end you'll figure out how you want to start. If all else fails, don't forget the basic questions."

"Basic questions? What do you mean?"

"*What* is one of them. Who, what, when, where, and why. Those question words are known as the five Ws—and sometimes you can add *how* to the list, too. If you answer all those questions, the story will write itself."

"Who . . ." It's so weird. I start to repeat the question words so I don't forget, but I get stuck on *who*. The next thing I know, I blurt out, "Who is Adam?"

The file open on my mother's lap slithers out of

her hands and onto the tile floor. We both watch it slip away from her fingers. Neither of us moves to pick up the papers that have escaped from the manila folder.

"Adam," Mom says, like she's been expecting this moment for years. "He was your dad's brother."

"Brother?" I'm not sure which of the five Ws I should use next. "What brother?"

Mom sighs, like she's too tired to go into it just now.

"Maybe we should get your father in here."

"Why?" I'm burning through my question words now. "Why didn't you tell me I have an Uncle Adam? What's wrong with him? Where is he?" Up until right now I thought Dad only had a younger sister, my Auntie Pam. She lives in England, not very far away from Nana.

"We didn't tell you because you don't have an uncle."

"But, you said—"

"Adam died when he was nineteen. He was seven years older than your father."

"So Dad was twelve when his brother died?" I let this sink in. I'm twelve. What would it be like if something happened to Matt?

"What happened? How did he die? Was he sick?"

"No. No. I never met him, but from everything I have heard, he was a very strong, smart, athletic young man. He died in a boating accident two days after he had been accepted at medical school. So, now you know."

The spell that holds us rigid in our seats breaks and Mom bends over to pick up the dropped papers.

Matt walks into Mom's office with Dolce, his favourite cockatiel, perched on his shoulder. I jump out of the chair.

"I was just leaving."

"Mom, can you help me clip Dolce's wings and trim her beak and toenails?" He is intent on his bird and doesn't pay any attention to me. Mia yips indignantly when I step on her toe. I have no idea when she crept into the room, but I shriek and we all laugh in surprise.

Dolce fluffs up her feathers and glares with sharp, black eyes at the dog. Mia slinks out into the hall like she's the one who did something wrong and then follows me up to my room.

Upstairs, I sprawl on my bed and stare at the boxes. Mia curls up on the floor by the bed and sighs.

"Heather?" My dad taps gently on the door.

"Come in."

"Hi, star reporter. Just thought I'd see if you needed any help with your story."

He looks exactly like the same dad I had at supper. Same short grey and white beard, same bony knees sticking out from his hollow boat shorts, same smiling brown eyes. The difference is now I know his secret. I'm not sure why that makes me feel guilty.

Mom couldn't have had time to tell him anything, so I don't let on that I know about Adam. My father's dead brother.

"I'm going to find some of my reference books. . . ."

He follows my glance over to the jumble of boxes.

"Are you ever going to unpack?" he asks.

"Maybe. One day."

"I'm sure you'd feel a lot more . . . comfortable here if you put some of your things on the shelves. I could probably bribe Matt to help you."

"No way! I don't want him touching my stuff!"

"Okay, okay! I was just trying to be helpful."

"Thanks."

"So, you don't need any help?"

"No. I mean, no thank you."

"Well, good luck!" Dad winks and backs out of the room.

I have no intention of unpacking anything since I have no intention of staying here. I'll just dig around in my boxes enough to find my dictionary and thesaurus. Somewhere, I even have books filled with quotes and quite a few about how to write. Those are more for poets and novelists, rather than newspaper reporters.

I start pawing through all my junk without actually unpacking. It takes me nearly an hour, but finally I find the reference books I need. By the time I do I've pushed all thoughts of whatever happened to Adam to a very distant corner of my brain. I have to concentrate, or I'll never get the article done by tomorrow and my career as a reporter will be over before it starts.

I open my thesaurus and start looking. Sometimes it helps me get going if I look up words related to what I'm writing about.

"Shipwreck." There are lots of words in the thesaurus like "smash," "shatter," "shiver," and "pulverize." None of them really apply to what happened to us.

I try "hunger" and find "famish," "starve," "be ravenous," and "have an aching void."

I could never have imagined that going on a sailing trip with my dad and brother would end up with me having an aching void.

Aching void. What a funny term. I flip through the dictionary, looking for inspiration. From between the pages, a handmade card flutters out. I pick it up and turn it over in my hands. The card is made from construction paper and on the front is a drawing of two girls and a house.

The drawing is just like you'd expect from a little kid. The girls in the picture both have on triangle-shaped dresses and have red bows ploinked on the tops of their heads. The bows look like figure eights. I don't need to open the card to know who made it. Maggie. We made each other friendship cards when we were in grade two. Somewhere, Maggie has one that I made for her.

I lie back on my pillow with the card resting on my tummy. I imagine that way across the country in Toronto, Maggie is lying on her bed, just like this, holding the card I made for her. All of a sudden I know exactly what an aching void feels like because I have one right in the pit of my stomach. Except the feeling has nothing whatsoever to do with being hungry.

I close my eyes and try to picture Maggie's face but the features are fuzzy and I start getting scared that maybe I've forgotten what she looks like. I don't know how it happens, but I guess I must be pretty tired because I fall asleep on my bed with all my clothes on still holding onto her card. The worst part is, I still haven't written a whole paragraph, never mind an article.

Chapter Nine

Collected Quote #17
I put a sheet of paper under my pillow, and when I could not sleep I wrote in the dark.—Henry David Thoreau
Source: Becca, Camp counsellor who tried to convince us to keep nature journals at summer camp

The strangest thing happened last night. In the middle of the night I sat up in the dark and I felt like if I just started, I could write the article. I turned on my little desk lamp and wrote non-stop until the whole thing was done. First thing this morning Mom and I took the story over to Mr. Turnbull's office. He read it on the spot, and he liked it! Not only that, he said that any time I wanted to write more stories for the paper I should let him know. I can't wait until Wednesday so I can see what my words look like in print!

Dad seems to be just as excited about my article as I am. If Mom repeated any part of our conversation from the day before, he isn't letting on. So, I don't say anything either.

"Heather, I think we should get to work on the writing cottage," he says when Mom and I get out of the car after we get back from dropping off the story.

The job of cleaning out the chicken coop is a lot more disgusting than either of us expected. Dad fights his way through the prickly mass of blackberry vines with an axe. An axe! He looks like he's hacking his way into the jungle. I'm right behind him when he stops in the doorway and lets his breath out slowly.

"We'd better wear masks," he says finally. When he moves out of the way to let me look inside, I can see why. I don't think the chicken coop was ever cleaned out. There are at least ten centimetres of chicken droppings, dirt, and old shavings on the floor. No wonder the rats were happy.

"And gloves," he adds.

We each put on one of Mom's surgical masks and haul away fourteen wheelbarrows full of stinky stuff before lunch.

"The vegetable garden will be happy," Dad says. We moved too late in the season to plant much of anything, but Dad has this idea that he is going to grow enough vegetables for us all to eat. He also wants to do a series of paintings called "Portraits of the Spirit Feeders." He says that's because when you grow your own food you don't just feed your body, you feed your spirit, too.

To make sure his vegetables will be the best specimens around, he started building raised beds, like gigantic boxes on the ground, where the plants will go in the spring.

We mix all the chicken manure into the big compost bins. By the time we break for lunch, Dad looks pretty happy but very tired.

"We can't quit now," I say.

"Were you reading my mind?"

"Dad . . . we've just started."

"Why don't you work in the tree this afternoon and we'll do some more in the morning?"

Writing in trees was fine for the first couple of weeks, but they are not exactly the most comfortable work environment. I keep dropping things. It's very disruptive to have to climb down out of my perch every time I drop my pen, which is often.

"Or why don't you keep going by yourself?"

I can tell Dad is just dying to play with the compost piles now that we've added all that manure.

"I'd like to turn the piles over, water them, cover them up."

I am beginning to feel like a mind reader.

"Fine. Maybe Matt will help me."

But Matt and Mom are wiring a cover over the top of one of the dog runs so Barnaby (that's what Matt named the Canada goose) has somewhere to recover from surgery. Mom set his wing and she figures Barnaby will be completely fine once it heals. After that, Matt has to do some reading practice, so that means he won't be available any time soon.

I find Mia who is innocently snoozing by the back porch. Actually, Mia has one eye open and watches Mathilde studiously washing her face with her soft, white paw. The dog knows better than to chase the cats, but the cats don't seem to understand about playing fair. As Mathilde distracts Mia's front end, Tony stalks the dog's silky tail. I arrive just in time to save Mia from a surprise attack from the rear and together we wander down to the end of the driveway to check the mail.

"Hi, Heather."

It's impossible to ignore Alyssum. She's swinging upside down from a tree branch at the side of the road, waiting for the mail truck. Her skirts flop and flap and she has to hold them up to keep them from hiding her face. Underneath, she is wearing bright purple tights. I can't understand why she wears so many layers when it's the middle of summer. Maybe her family is so poor they don't have any heat and it takes all day to warm up after a long night of shivering.

That's when I get my brilliant idea. If Allan Turnbull wants more articles from me, maybe he would like to publish one about the poor families of Tarragon Island. In my head I'm already planning how I could write one of those feature articles that tells all about a particular social problem. I could use our neighbours as the focus so I get all the facts straight. As a bonus, I'll also be gathering details for my novel about poverty and despair.

Nobody will know that Rose in the novel is based on Alyssum in real life, even though both girls are named after flowers. Alyssum swings back and forth from her knees. Her arms flop down towards the ground and her skirts (today one is bright blue with swirls of white and the other is white with tiny green flowers) flap down and hide her face. That doesn't stop her from talking.

"My mom says it's okay if you come over to play," she says.

This is a great opportunity to see first-hand what goes on inside the home of a poor family.

"Sure," I agree.

"But not today. The twins are napping. And anyway, first I want to come over to your place because my dad says your mom's vet clinic is right inside your house. Can I see it?"

"Twins?"

"Robert and Eric. They're just babies."

I've never met real twins before. "Can you tell them apart?"

"Of course." Alyssum pushes her skirts up and stares at me like I'm a bit stupid.

"Is it fun having twins?"

Alyssum doesn't seem any more impressed with

this question than my last one.

"Twice as much trouble. Twice as much noise."

She changes the subject. It's pretty obvious she is not happy about having twins at her house.

"What are you doing today? Can I come over now?"

"Well . . . actually I am kind of busy. I'm busy fixing up my writing cottage."

"You're a writer?" She wrinkles her nose. It's hard to tell what she thinks about that.

Alyssum kicks her feet out and flips over. She lands on her feet in the soft grass. Her face is flushed a deep red. Sandy bounds down the driveway and Mia bounces up and down on her back legs like a long-haired rabbit, she's so excited to see the other dog.

"Do you need some help? Fixing the cottage, I mean?"

She doesn't look like she would be much use to anybody, she's so small. "How old are you?"

Alyssum's eyes flash. "What do you mean, how old am I? What does it matter to you?"

"Sorry! I was just curious. . . ." I couldn't exactly say that I thought she was too young to help.

"I'm ten."

I bite my tongue before I say, "You're kidding!" She sure doesn't look ten, she's so small. When I think about it, though, it sort of makes sense. Poor people can't afford good quality food so their kids probably don't grow as big as other people's.

"Would you like a muffin? My brother baked some last night."

"Your brother?"

I nod. Matt loves to cook. "Chocolate chip muffins are his specialty." Her eyes light up and I wonder if she's had any breakfast.

July 27 Sitting on the floor in my new writing cottage.

Today Alyssum came over. She is the kind of girl who

asks a lot of questions. She wanted to know if Dad was a vet, why we have a Canada goose in the dog runs and if we have a composting toilet. They do. A composting toilet? I can't imagine what their house must smell like. I feel very sorry for her because her family obviously can't even afford running water in the bathroom. I bet they have to bring water from a well and maybe they don't even have electricity.

I told her we have a flushing toilet and her response was, "Do you know how much water you waste every time you flush?" I guess they must be careful with every drop they use since their well is probably away from the house and it must take a long time for them to carry enough buckets to the house to fill a bathtub. I wonder how they wash their clothes? Maybe in the river? I don't even know if that's legal. They probably go to the Laundromat in the village.

That's not really what I was going to write about in my journal today. I wanted to celebrate because this is the first thing I've written sitting inside my writing cottage. Alyssum may ask a lot of questions, but boy, can she work. We hosed down and scrubbed the walls, then we cut down the rest of the wild blackberries and weeds and cut a proper path up to the door. Dad said we couldn't use the lawnmower so that meant we had to cut the grass with hand clippers.

Tomorrow we're going to paint everything and Mom said she has some fabric so we can make curtains. It already looks very cozy and I'm just sitting on the floor!

While we were working, Alyssum asked if I wanted to help her at the stand her family has at the Saturday market. She said if I baked some cookies or made jam I could sell my stuff there. I said I wanted to earn some money to buy special journals and fancy pens, but of course, every penny I earn will go into my bus fund. I wonder how long the paper will take to pay me my five bucks?

Chapter Ten

Collected Quote #72
When I am working on a book or a story I write every morning as soon after the first light as possible. There is no one to disturb you and it is cool or cold and you come to your work and warm as you write.—Ernest Hemingway
Source: Mr. Helliwell, Grade 6 Language Arts teacher

I never get up early voluntarily. That's why it's so strange to be sitting here on the floor in "Dove Cottage." Dad told me that in lots of places people name their houses and cottages. He also told me that the poet, William Wordsworth, lived in a place called Dove Cottage. Since this used to be a place for birds (though chickens aren't as poetic as doves), it seemed like a good name.

This morning, I couldn't sleep in, even though I pulled the blankets over my head. Instead of making me sleepy, being in my blanket cave was really hot and I thought I would suffocate. Then I started thinking about Dove Cottage and the novel about poverty and despair. I need a name for that, too. I wrote some possible titles in my journal.

—Desperate Vision: A Story of a Girl Who Dreams of Escaping the Bonds of Poverty
—The Slum-dwellers

—Rose the Rag-picker
—Poor, Poor Rosie Brown

Sometimes, if I write down a whole list of titles, one of them jumps out at me as being just right. I think I like "Poor, Poor Rosie Brown," or "Poor Rosie" for short. Even though I've been trying to work since just after dawn, I'm not getting very far.

More Observations of Alyssum (Rosie)

The problem is, I have way more questions about how poor people live than I have observations. I mean, I know that Alyssum isn't lazy like Matt. She seemed to enjoy hosing out the chicken coop. Probably that's because she has to do things like bake bread from scratch. She told me about that. Alyssum and her mom make things like fancy braided bread to sell at the market. The thing is, I'm too worried about hurting her feelings and so I don't ask all the questions I want to ask.

Maybe when she gets here today to help paint I can lead the conversation around to find out more details of her life. In the meantime, I guess I can work on "Poor Rosie," and then fill in the details once I have more facts.

"Heather?"

My heart thuds in my chest like a little bird trying to burst out of me. My eyes are open but I still can't quite see where I am. I have this panicky feeling that I've gone blind except I know that can't be true because I can see things. It's just that my bed is gone and everything looks very peculiar—dusty and dim.

"Heather?"

I can't figure out why Alyssum is in my house. Then the door of the chicken coop slams open and she's standing in the doorway looking down at me where I'm lying on the dirt floor.

"Hi. I guess I fell asleep."

She doesn't even think that's strange. At least, she doesn't say anything about how odd it is that I'm snoozing in a chicken coop.

"Where's the paint? Your mom said I could watch her in the clinic after we've finished. So, let's get going. Your mom's really nice."

"You were talking to my mother?"

Even though I'm totally awake now, my brain is still not quite keeping up with the conversation.

"Yeah, your mother. She said you left a note on the breakfast table saying you were working at Dove Cottage. That's a pretty name. Now, where's the paint?"

The paint tins are beside the door and Alyssum gets right down to business. "I'm guessing this screwdriver is for the lids?"

I can't answer because I have no clue why you would need a screwdriver to paint. Alyssum seems to know more than I do because as I watch, she jams the tip of the screwdriver under the lip of the paint can and pries off the top. She steps outside, snaps a branch of the plum tree, and strips off the leaves.

"What are you doing?"

"We have to stir the paint first."

"Oh. Right."

"There, let's get to work." She hands me a paint-brush and we start on the end wall.

"These brushes are way too small," she says after about fifteen minutes. We've both been painting pretty quickly, but we've only covered a tiny bit of the wall. "Don't you have anything better?"

I have no idea so we go and find Dad. He's sitting under a tree with a huge sail spread out on the ground in front of him. He has a long, curvy needle in his hand and he's stitching a patch onto the sail.

"This is Alyssum from next door," I say. "She was wondering if we have any bigger brushes."

"You're not trying to paint the coop with those little brushes I put by the paint cans, are you?"

"I thought that's what they were there for."

Dad laughs. "You'll be painting from now until Christmas if you use those! No, the small brushes are to do the lettering on your sign."

"Sign?" Alyssum sounds confused.

"I figured you'd want to make a 'Dove Cottage' sign. The big brushes are in the shed. On the shelf by the lifejackets."

"You have a boat?" Alyssum asks when we lift up the life jackets and find two huge house-painting brushes.

"A sailboat called *Ariel*."

"Really? I love to sail!"

"You do?" It's hard to imagine anyone enjoying sailing. I've only been sailing once—the trip to Billy's Cove hardly counts. That was on Lake Ontario with my best friend Maggie's family. The whole time we were out on the water, I thought the boat was going to tip over. It took forever to get anywhere because we couldn't sail in a straight line; we had to zig zag back and forth depending on where the wind was coming from.

"Especially in the winter when the wind comes up. One of my friends lives on a sailboat and sometimes I go sailing with them. Once we even went in a race around the island. That's part of the Wild Rose Festival."

"Wild Rose Festival?"

"At the end of the summer—the last weekend of summer holidays. There's a livestock fair, pie-eating contests, the round-the-island sailboat race, and tons of other stuff. It's lots of fun! You'll love it!"

"Well, I'm not sure if I'll be here."

"You're going away?"

"Maybe." I don't feel like telling her about my travel plans. I don't know her well enough to tell her a secret as important as that. "I'll race you back to Dove Cottage!"

The distraction works. She may be only ten years old, but can Alyssum ever run fast! We reach the door of the cottage at exactly the same time.

By lunch, we have finished both ends and the back wall of Dove Cottage. The painting didn't take long at all once we had the proper brushes.

"Hungry?"

Alyssum nods so we head up to the house to find something to eat.

"Doesn't your mom cook you a lunch?" Alyssum asks when I dig out the grilled cheese sandwich maker and start assembling the bread and cheese.

"Nope. She's lucky some days if she gets a lunch break herself. Most of the time Dad makes her a sandwich and takes it into the clinic."

Alyssum stares down the hall towards the closed door leading to the clinic. "I wish I could watch her," she says longingly.

"Do you want some chili?" I ask when I spot a bowl of leftovers in the fridge.

"Does it have meat in it?"

I nod.

"No, thank you. I'm a vegetarian."

"You don't eat any meat?"

She shakes her head and gulps down some orange juice.

"Not even hot dogs?"

"We buy tofu dogs. I like them with ketchup and mustard."

Since Mom and Dad are always complaining about the price of meat and we barely ever eat steak,

I guess it makes sense that Alyssum's family never eats meat. I can't imagine how awful that must be.

"Not even salami or ham sandwiches? What about pepperoni pizza?"

"We *do* eat dairy products, so there's tons of choices for sandwiches and pizza. My aunt's family are vegans. They don't eat any dairy products at all—nothing that comes from animals."

"What about eggs?"

"Nope. Eggs come from chickens. Chickens are animals."

"Isn't that incredibly boring?"

Again she gives me that look which clearly says, "Boy, are you dumb." My skin prickles a bit whenever she does that. But it's not my fault. Until a minute ago, I'd never even heard the word *vegan*.

"You should come over to my house for dinner sometime."

"It's okay," I say quickly. I can just imagine what it would be like for them to have to find the extra money to feed a guest. But then I notice Alyssum is staring at the floor and biting her bottom lip. She seems very disappointed. "Well, maybe I could. If it's okay with your parents."

Alyssum brightens up when I say that.

"Hi, girls."

"Dr. Blake!"

My mom laughs. "Call me Bobbi."

"Bobbi?" Alyssum looks a bit bewildered. "That's a boy's name."

"Short for Roberta. Who would want to go through life with a name like 'Roberta'? Not me! Why don't you come and join me after you've finished your lunch? I have a couple of people coming in with their animals for vaccinations. Nothing too exciting, but if you'd like to watch . . ."

"Oh, yes, please!"

I guess I've lost my painting assistant for the rest of the afternoon. Not that I care. I was really only letting her help so I could learn more about her anyway. Alyssum trots off after my mother asking a string of questions. "Have you ever been bitten by a dog? Is it true you can use an anaesthetic on a bird? How do you make them breathe it in? Or do you give them a shot to make them go to sleep? How did you make the Canada goose sleep when you fixed his wing?"

My mom laughs and answers all the questions just as fast as Alyssum can ask them. Their chatting stops when they close the clinic door, as if someone had turned off the volume. I know that all I have to do is get up, go down the hall, and follow them into the clinic, but somehow when the door closes it's like they shut me out on purpose.

Chapter Eleven

Collected Quote # 16
Almost anyone can be an author; the business is to
collect money and fame from this state of being.
—A.A. Milne
Source: Charlie

Alyssum stays in the clinic with Mom for ages. I hang
out in the kitchen, making notes and waiting for Dad
and Matt to come home.

"You're famous!" Matt bursts into the kitchen
waving a newspaper around. "Dad and I picked up ten
copies in town. You can send them to your friends
and Granny and Grandpa and start a scrapbook. . . ."

"Let me see!"

And there, right on the front page of the July 28
edition of the *Tarragon Times,* is my story.

I study the story and then I read it again and
again. I lean against the fridge and feel almost like I'm
going to faint. My name, Heather Blake, is right on
the front page of the paper. The paper shakes in my
hands and when Dad comes into the kitchen, my face
feels like it's going to split in half, I'm smiling so
hard.

"The photograph looks great, doesn't it?" Dad
says, teasing. "And the article isn't bad, either."

"We're celebrities," boasts Matt. "We were at the

grocery store and the lady at the checkout recognized us!" Matt bounces up and down on his toes. "Then the man behind us in the lineup said the story was really good. He wanted to know if you were going to be a regular reporter!"

Matt looks so proud, as if he has written the story himself.

Local Family Stranded on Sailboat
by Heather Blake

On July 25, Heather Blake, her brother, Matt, and her father, Ben, had a very harrowing experience. Heather's father, a city slicker through and through, recently moved to Tarragon Island from Toronto to commune with nature. Last week, he decided to take his two kids for a sail on the family boat, *Ariel*.

Ben, an inexperienced mariner, took his boat out without going through routine safety checks. *Ariel* didn't have emergency fuel, food, water or a working radio! Disaster struck the unfortunate trio when they tried to return from their picnic destination, Billy's Cove. As they were getting ready to come home after a pleasant outing, they discovered an empty gas can and lack of sustenance. As luck would have it, Ben had overlooked a very important rule—he hadn't told anyone where they had planned to go, which made it very difficult for coast guard searchers to find them!

Heather, 12, and Matt, 9, rowed their dinghy ashore to look for help while Ben guarded the boat and meagre supplies. Just as the kids were getting tired, hungry, cold and scared, they saw something in even worse trouble than they were! Upon investigation, they found a thrashing Canada goose with a broken wing. Luckily, Matt, a boy who is very good with animals, knew what to do. The Blake kids took the goose (now known as Barnaby) back to *Ariel*.

The foursome spent an uncomfortable night on the boat before being spotted by a coast guard boat that had been alerted by veterinarian Bobbi Blake. Dr. Blake had become worried when her loving but incapable husband had not returned in time for dinner and she suspected he might have run into a bit of trouble.

Though very hungry, her family returned unharmed. Barnaby the goose is recovering in Dr. Blake's clinic.

"Congratulations, Heather." My dad pats a kitchen chair and smiles at me. "Though next time you'd like to make a fool of someone, would you mind choosing someone else?" Dad winks at me so I know he isn't seriously upset. "Otherwise, it's a great story!"

I feel so incredibly, deliciously, deliriously happy I

can hardly stand it. I float across the kitchen and sink into the chair. I'm so stunned and pleased and proud and excited that before I even get halfway through my muffin I find myself picking up the phone and dialing the number for the paper.

"Hello, Mr. Turnbull please?" My voice quavers, and Dad ruffles my hair, winks, and heads back outside.

A moment later the editor comes on the line.

"Thank you for putting my story in the paper." I take a deep breath to try to control my shaky voice. "Do you think you might be interested in another story?"

"Absolutely! What do you have in mind?"

I launch into my idea, tripping and stumbling over my words. "I know there are lots of poor people around, even here on the island, and I was thinking I could write a real-life dramatic story about how hard it is to struggle with being poor and not having enough money for nice clothes and stuff like that and especially what other people think about you if you are poor . . . and . . ."

I have to stop to take a breath and then I get all worried because at the other end of the line there is complete silence.

"Hello? Are you still there?" This is a dumb idea, I think. What am I doing calling a busy editor who is probably trying to think of a good way to let me down without hurting my feelings. . . .

"Poverty on Tarragon Island, hmm? Interesting."

He doesn't sound at all convinced that there is anything interesting about the subject.

"Or maybe not—if you think I should write about something else . . ."

"Well, wait just a minute. Let's talk about this. What makes you think poverty is a big problem here?"

"Well, I happen to . . ." I look around the corner and into the hall, but the door to the clinic is shut and there is no sign of Alyssum. Just to be on the safe side, I lower my voice. "I met someone who is very poor and I'm kind of observing her life. I thought I would base the story on what I learn."

"I see."

"Unless you think I should do something else . . ."

The longer this phone conversation goes on, the worse I feel. Now I'm so nervous I wish I hadn't eaten any of that muffin because my stomach is flipping over and over and my hands are sweating so much I have to pinch the receiver between my neck and shoulder and wipe my palms on my jeans.

"Poverty is a pretty serious subject," Mr. Turnbull says finally. "Are you sure you want to tackle something like this?"

At this point, I'm not sure of anything. Just then I hear the door open in the hallway and I start gulping for air. All my happiness has completely evaporated. "Sure. When would you like it?"

"Before the Wild Rose Festival. That gives you a little more than a month. Is that enough time?"

I nod foolishly and realize that he can't see me. "Yes. Sure."

We hang up and I turn around to see Alyssum standing in the doorway looking very pale.

"What's the matter?" I feel horribly guilty, like she knows I've been spying on her.

"This cat came in and his one leg was all scraped bare because he got hit by a car and you could see the muscles and the skin. . . ."

"Sit down."

I know what she's going through. That's why I don't help in the clinic very often.

I pour her a tall glass of lemonade. "Here, drink

this. If he didn't get hit in the head, he'll probably survive."

Alyssum gulps down the drink. "Except maybe the owners won't know where to find him."

"Don't worry. Mom's really good about finding people. She puts up posters when strays come in, lets the paper know—and every week she gives a list to the RCMP. A lot of people call the police when their pets go missing."

In Toronto, she also worked with the local SPCA and the city pound, but here there's no pound and not even an SPCA office.

"Are you okay now?"

She nods and then pushes her lips together and stands up.

"You're going back in there?"

"If I'm going to be a vet, I have to get past my . . ."

"Revulsion?" I offer. It's a good word but she looks faintly disgusted.

"Inexperience," she counters and marches boldly back down the hall. I hear her take a very deep breath before she opens the door to the clinic and disappears again.

Then it's my turn to start fretting. *What have I done now?* It was hard enough to write a simple "who, what, when, where, why" story about a little boating mishap. *How on earth am I going to manage to write a long, serious piece about poverty?*

Dove Cottage seems like a good place to go and think. I drag my desk chair and several large packing boxes outside and proceed to furnish my new office. By the time I have moved everything around three times, tacked up some flowery fabric over the window, dragged an extension cord from the house to the cottage, and convinced Dad I'm not going to set the place on fire if I have a lamp on my makeshift box desk, I need a tall glass of lemonade myself. Of course, I haven't written a single word.

While I'm sipping my icy cold drink, I comfort myself by reading my article in the paper. If I could do it once, I tell myself firmly, I can do it again.

Chapter Twelve

Collected Quote #88
Writing is not a profession but a vocation of unhappiness.
—Georges Simenon
Source: Never Give Up: Encouraging Words for Writers,
by Jake Stanley

On Friday, two exciting things arrive at our place. The first is a letter from Maggie. The other is a strange-looking baby cow called Chelsea.

"Matt, meet Chelsea. Chelsea, meet Matt. She's a Dexter heifer." Mom beams at Matt.

"Heifer?"

"She's a girl. Girl calves are called heifers."

The black heifer has unbelievably short legs. Her ears stick out sideways from her broad head like stubby airplane propeller blades. Mia looks up at the newcomer, her whole body quivering. I suppose she thinks the cow is a new playmate.

"Is she mine?" Matt bounces up and down and then he stops, walks slowly to Chelsea, and holds out his hand to her broad wet nose. Chelsea's thick, dark tongue slurps out and gives him a good lick. Mom nods. She stands behind Matt and puts both her hands on his shoulders.

"If you promise to keep working on your reading, you can take her in the livestock show at the Wild Rose Festival."

Matt is so pleased with himself his cheeks puff out and he looks taller than his usual self.

He cranes his head up to look at Mom and she leans forward and kisses him on the forehead. "Deal?"

"Deal," he agrees.

While Mom, Dad, and Matt are getting Chelsea settled into the barn, I head for Dove Cottage to deal with my correspondence. I reread Maggie's letter for the tenth time.

Dear Heather,

Thank you for all your letters. I'm sorry I haven't written sooner. I've started about a thousand letters to you but none of them were as good as talking to you—you know what I mean?

I miss you I miss you I miss you I miss you. But, enough moping and complaining! This letter I'm really going to finish and then I'm really going to mail it.

The writing group just isn't the same without you. Remember that short story Racquel was writing about the boy in the barn who finds the strange box of coins buried under some hay? Guess what? She won a prize in the library's short story contest. She won some books and four passes to Black Creek Pioneer Village!!!!!!!!!

Her mom took me, Racquel, Anna and Toni. Toni is a new girl who just moved here. She joined the writing group after you left. Toni's really funny and writes all these crazy songs that make us nearly bust our guts laughing. You've been to the Black Creek Pioneer Village, right? The place with all the old fashioned buildings and people dressed up in olden days clothing and farm animals and everything?

We had a lot of fun because we went on a wagon ride pulled by the hugest horse you have ever seen. I was allowed to go because I'm still trying to finish the story about the Gold Rush and I need to know accurate stuff about pioneer life.

On the way back we stopped at the Willowdale Mall and I bought a new pair of Kelly Jeans. I love them!

Have you seen your school yet? Pinkey says hi. Do you have a new best friend? Please don't tell me if you do because my heart will break, my BBFP (that stands for Bestest Buddy and Forever Pal).

Write soon. You should get e-mail and then I wouldn't have to wait so long to get a letter back from you. Is that Island of yours still stuck in the middle ages?

Your BBFP,
Maggie

Getting the letter makes me want to cry. I can just see Maggie sitting at her old fashioned rolltop desk writing to me with her cat, Pinkey, sitting on her papers, batting at the end of the pen with his paw.

Maggie and I were the original members of the North Hill Writing Group. The writing group used to meet every Tuesday after school. Maggie loves stuff from the olden days and most of her stories are set back in pioneer times. I always used to tease her that she was really Laura Ingalls Wilder reincarnated to write the *Little House on the Prairie* books that Laura didn't have a chance to finish.

After we had been meeting for about six months, Anna Tremblay started coming to meetings with her poetry. Then Racquel Owens joined the group. At first Racquel was really shy and didn't want to read us any of her stories and then one day she got brave and read us this story about a girl who wakes up one morning and discovers somebody left a baby on the front steps of her house.

That's the kind of story Racquel likes to write. Creepy. Mysterious. Her characters always have deep secrets that you can't figure out until right at the end. It doesn't surprise me that she won a prize. I wish I could feel proud. But I don't. I feel really mean inside, and a voice keeps chanting in my head, "Why won't anyone publish my poems?"

The worst part about Maggie's letter is reading about Toni. I wonder if Toni is a better writer than I am? I bet she wants to be Maggie's best friend. It's easy to be Maggie's best friend because she is so funny and pretty and easy to get along with. It's not fair at all that Toni, a complete stranger, can just move to Toronto, take over my place in the group, and steal my best friend at the same time.

I don't want to be, but when I sit down to write a letter back to Maggie I'm really angry and I press so hard on the paper the pen pushes right through and makes a hole! I close my eyes and try to picture Maggie and Pinkey and the rolltop desk and then start again.

Dear Mags,
  Your trip to Black Creek Village sounds like it was fun. I guess you got lots of ideas about Gold Rush days. We don't have anything like that around here—Black Creek, I mean.

I know I should say something nice about Racquel's prize.

  Say congratulations to Racquel. That's really great that she won!

I wonder if Maggie was jealous, too. She knows me so well, maybe she'll be able to tell I'm not exactly dancing up and down with joy, no matter what I write.

  Mom says we will have e-mail by the time school starts. Things are still kind of disorganized around here. I've driven past my school and once I looked into the windows but everything is locked up for the summer. It's small, only one story, and there's only one grade 7

90

class—not five like at home.

At home. Where the North Hill Writing Group meets every Tuesday. I chew on the end of my pen and consider what to say next.

Please don't say anything, but I might actually be coming back in the fall. I guess maybe I still wouldn't be going to school with you because I'm going to live with my grandparents in Guelph, but at least I'll get to see you sometimes.

I try to imagine what the writing group is like now that Toni has joined. Does she sit in my regular chair at Maggie's house? What a horrible thought.

Are you best friends with Toni?

I scratch out the last part about Toni and bite the inside of my cheek. It's really hard to think of something nice to write.

Is Toni really funny? I'm glad you found somebody else to join the writing group. Four was a good number of people.

Maggie. Racquel. Anna. And Heather. That's what the fourth name should be. Not dumb, funny Toni. It's a major effort to tear my brain out of miserable gear, but I figure I can't end my letter without saying something positive.

I have some good news, too. We went out on our boat and I wrote an article about it. I'll enclose a copy so you can see I'm not kidding. So far, no luck on getting the kitchen poem published. I'll keep trying. I sent it out to a magazine called "Crack Pots." I sure hope they like it. I'm working on another article right now about poverty on Tarragon Island. It's hard to write about real things.

Harder than making up stories, I think.

   Oh, I almost forgot. I'm not writing to you from my room. I'm sitting in Dove Cottage—my own private studio/workshop/office place. It used to be

I stop for a second. I don't want the world to know I'm working in a former chicken coop. Shed? Shack? Small barn? Then it comes to me . . .

a rustic outbuilding that we have renovated. I'll send you a picture.

Write back soon.

Don't forget me.

   Forever and ever your best friend in the world,
                    Heather xoxoxoxoxo

P.S. Matt got a calf, I mean a heifer, called Chelsea
P.S. #2 You're so lucky you got Kelly Jeans! There's only one small clothing shop here on the island and they don't have any cool clothes at all!

   I lick the back of the envelope and then cough to stop myself from crying. It's crazy to cry. I'll be seeing everybody again very soon. Just as soon as I have enough for my bus ticket out of here.

Chapter Thirteen

Collected Quote #33
Nothing you write, if you hope to be any good, will ever come out as you first hoped.—Lillian Hellman
Source: Charlie, after Marion Alsworthy told me to rewrite the kitchen poem

"That's very responsible of you, Heather."

Mom sounds very impressed that instead of just spending my money from the newspaper right away, I want to open a savings account at the bank. I just wish I weren't lying to her about why I'm suddenly so interested in saving. Well, I didn't exactly lie. I told her that someday I might like to go travelling. I suppose she thinks sometime after I finish high school and not in a few short weeks at the end of the summer, but it's not really my fault that she misinterpreted what I told her.

I must admit that when I'm finally finished filling out all the forms at the bank I'm pretty impressed myself that I deposited the whole five dollars into my new account. Normally, if I have money it barely has time to get used to the inside of my pocket and I've already spent it three times over! Maybe I've just never had a reason to save up before now.

When Matt said we were celebrities, he sure wasn't kidding. This morning, for example, at least twelve people talked to me about being marooned. One man, the guy who owns the little marina, actually offered to pay any costs associated with saving Barnaby! I felt like a hero when the lady at the ice cream stand wouldn't let me pay for my cone.

"Welcome to Tarragon Island," she said. "We love it when new writers and artists move here."

I was too embarrassed to ask her what she meant about that. Maybe it's such a stupid place to live that when, occasionally, somebody vaguely interesting moves here everybody gets excited. I figure they have to be desperate if they start treating some kid who's only ever published one article in a real paper like a superstar.

Mom says that's just another reason why living here is so great. "People know who you are," she says. "In a small town, your successes are everyone's successes."

I feel kind of bad for my dad, though. One guy at the marina offered to give him sailing lessons and another guy gave him an old radio and absolutely refused to take any money for it. "Don't look great, but it works good," is what he said. The worst part of that is, it's sort of my fault that the whole world knows my dad wasn't exactly prepared when he set out on the trip.

Actually, that's not quite the worst part. Dad doesn't like to look stupid any more than I do, so when he heard about the round-the-island race at the end of the summer, he decided to prove to everyone that what happened at Billy's Cove was a total accident.

"We'll show them, won't we? We'll win the darned race!"

"On *Ariel*?" My mom has to try very hard not to laugh when Dad brings up the whole subject of racing these days.

Face it, *Ariel* isn't exactly a sleek racing yacht. The sail my dad was patching is in about the best shape of the lot. But again, when Dad talks about the yacht race, there's a kind of challenge in his voice, like when he was convincing Mom that buying a boat was a good idea.

I guess there isn't anything so awful about Dad going in a boat race if he wants to, except he needs a crew and guess who he expects to sail with him? Yup. Me. And Matt.

I can hardly refuse since I'm the one who wrote all about his . . . his . . . incompetence in the paper. I've already promised myself that I'll write a story about our racing experience and I know that even if everything that could possibly go wrong does go wrong, the article will make Dad sound totally brilliant. That way, I'll never have to go sailing again and everybody will think Dad is great.

I mean, I'd hate to leave town without fixing the damage I've done. That doesn't seem quite right.

"Heather, can you help me give Chelsea a bath?"

"Didn't you see the sign?"

Matt pokes at the dirt outside Dove Cottage with the toe of his Wellington boot. He doesn't say anything, but it's too late. He has broken my concentration.

"The sign says, 'Please Do Not Disturb—Writer at Work.'"

"I know what it says. You've been in there all morning. I thought you might need a break."

"You're not serious about giving that calf a bath?"

"She's not a calf, she's a heifer."

"Whatever. Why does your heifer need a bath?"

"She has to get used to being handled so we can win at the Wild Rose Festival. Dad's going to help me

95

make a display about Dexter cattle. Did you know Chelsea's an endangered species?"

"She's a cow, for Pete's sake!" Sometimes Matt gets the craziest ideas in his head. "Cows can't be endangered. That's for Siberian tigers and stuff like that."

"Wrong again, oh great author. You should do some research. Mom told me all about Dexters and other rare breeds of farm animals."

He clamps his mouth shut so I can see there's no way I'm going to find out anything more about endangered cows from Matt because I've hurt his feelings.

"Okay, I'll help you if you help me."

Matt regards me suspiciously. "Help you do what?"

"Tomorrow is Saturday and I said I'd help Alyssum at her market stall."

"Doing what?"

"Baking."

"You're helping her bake?"

Sometimes having a conversation with Matt is so exasperating. "No. She's baking at her house and I'm supposed to make cookies here. Then, tomorrow morning, I'm going with her and we'll both sell our baked goods at the market."

"Do you get to keep your money?"

"Of course. But it's going straight in the bank so don't think you can ask for a loan or anything."

"I still don't get how you are helping Alyssum. It sounds like she's the one helping *you* by giving you a place to sell your stuff. Are you paying her rent?"

"Rent?"

"If you had a store, you'd have to pay somebody rent."

I wish I hadn't mentioned the whole baking thing because now I'm thinking that I probably should have offered to pay something for my corner of Alyssum's table. "I'll pay my way," I say.

"How?"

"Never mind. That's between me and Alyssum. Can you help me with a recipe for cookies or not?"

Matt looks more than a little smug since he is the one who cooks and bakes. I'm so stupid in the kitchen I don't bother making toast in the morning since I usually manage to burn it.

"Yeah, sure, I guess so. As long as you don't make me eat anything you cook. I want to live to see the end of the summer."

He jumps out of the way when I lunge forward to punch his arm. I chase him and then Mia appears out of nowhere, nips at his heels, and we all race to the barn. Matt stops suddenly in the doorway and it's all I can do not to plough right over him.

"What are you doing?"

"Shhhhhhh. You'll scare her. You have to move slowly."

He starts moving forward like he's in slow motion. "Easy, girl. Hi there, Chelsea."

There's an answering rustle from the first big stall in the barn. I peek over the stall door. Chelsea is standing quietly in the corner, chewing thoughtfully, her deep brown eyes gazing at Matt.

He takes a halter and rope from a hook outside the stall and then lets himself inside. He pulls a handful of grain from his pocket and Chelsea ambles across the stall and nuzzles at his hand to get at the treat. Obviously, Matt has done this before. He strokes the space between her eyes and then moves to her side. He slips the halter over her ears and buckles it up. Then they both look up at me.

"Come in and help me."

"What am I supposed to do?"

"Walk on her other side."

Leaving the stall door wide open, I take my position at the other side of Chelsea's head.

"Okay, girl, let's go."

Chelsea just stands there. She turns her head towards Matt and stares at him. "Chelsea, come on." He tugs on the lead rope fastened to her halter. "Come on, bath time."

The heifer seems to have other ideas. She plants her feet firmly and glares at the stall door.

"Mia! Look out!"

"She'll get trampled!" As soon as the words are out of my mouth I realize how stupid they sound. At the rate Chelsea is travelling, she isn't likely to trample anything.

"Get lost! Go home!" Mia just stands there in the open doorway of the stall, her eyebrows twitching up and down and her nostrils quivering. As far as she's concerned, she *is* at home. She licks her lips and whines.

"Grab the dog and stick her in one of the runs," Matt directs. I don't normally like to take instructions from my little brother, but in this case, it's clear Chelsea isn't going anywhere until the killer Yorkie is out of sight.

When I get back to the barn, Matt has already led his charge outside near the hose.

"How did you get her to move?"

He pats his pocket. "Bribery. You hold her while I wet her down."

"Yeah, right. She'll run away!"

"No she won't. That's why you're holding her. Here."

Matt scoops more grain out of his pocket and hands it to me. "Feed this to her a little bit at a time. That should distract her."

Matt turns on the tap and the hose twitches like it's coming to life. I stand on it so it doesn't spray all over me while I stand at Chelsea's head, feeding her grain a few morsels at a time. She looks very serious when she licks my fingers and the palm of my hand.

As Matt works, he talks to his cow non-stop. "Good girl, Chelsea. I'm going to spray under your tummy now . . . that's a gooooood girl. And now some shampoo . . ."

He squirts shampoo all over Chelsea's glistening back and begins to scrub. Chelsea doesn't pay any attention at all. She just stands there like her feet have grown into the ground. I keep feeding her grain, listening to Matt chatter on and on.

Back in Ontario he kept rabbits at Granny and Grandpa's farm. He belonged to the 4H Rabbit Club and went to rabbit shows during the summer holidays. He was always jealous of the kids who had goats, sheep, and cows.

"Did you hear the Cranwells are coming for dinner?"

"The who?"

"Cranwells. Our neighbours. You know, the ones with that girl who's helping you fix up the chicken coop."

"Dove Cottage. You mean Alyssum?"

"Yeah. Her parents are coming over for dinner tomorrow."

"Oh no!"

"What's wrong with that?"

"They don't eat meat! Does Mom know?"

Matt shrugs. "I guess so. They were talking on the phone for ages this morning."

"What about the twins?"

Another shrug. "How should I know?"

Sometimes Matt can be completely annoying. Like when he only knows half the story but makes it seem like he knows a lot more.

"They have twin babies over there. I want to see them."

"So go over to their house."

"I will. Tomorrow morning. When we have to load up to go to the market. So then they're coming here? After we come back from the market?"

Another shrug.

"Are we done yet?"

Matt squirts water over Chelsea's back, under her tummy, down her legs, rinsing away all the soap suds.

"I have to dry her off."

"What!"

"Mom gave me those old towels."

He starts rubbing a towel over Chelsea's neck. "You can't just leave her all wet. She'll get sick."

There's no point in being impatient. Matt never does anything by half measures. I can hardly walk off and just leave the cow standing there.

"Why can't we tie her up somewhere?"

"She's a lot stronger than she looks. She could hurt herself, or pull the fence over or—"

"You could tie her to a tree."

"No trees within reach of the hose. Besides, she likes you and psychologically, it's better for her to have company."

"Psychologically? Are you kidding? She's a cow!"

"Cows are herd animals. They don't like to be alone."

"What does that make me?"

Matt doesn't answer. He finishes his thought aloud. "I've been reading up on cows and how they think. I'm going to ask Mom and Dad if they'll buy a second cow."

"Another one?"

He nods. "Otherwise she'll get lonely." He stops towelling her off and comes to her head. He scratches behind one of her propeller ears and grins. "She's great, isn't she?"

He doesn't expect an answer, so I don't give him one. It isn't until much later that it hits me—Matt actually read something voluntarily. A book about how cows think. That's so weird, it's hard to believe we're related.

Chapter Fourteen

Collected Quote #38
The best time for planning a book is while you're doing the dishes.—Agatha Christie
Source: Finding Time to Write Your Novel, 3rd Edition

"Pay attention! They're burning!" Matt runs into the kitchen and rips open the oven door.

I yank out the cookie tray and it clatters to the counter top. The edges of the cookies are rather dark.

Matt flips one over with a spatula. "You can't sell these!"

He's right. Underneath, the cookies are completely black.

"You have to watch what you're doing!"

Just then the timer goes off on the oven. Matt continues his lecture before I can say anything.

"The timer is just a guide—once the oven gets hot, sometimes the cookies bake faster. You have to keep an eye on them. Didn't you smell them burning? What were you doing in here?"

I can't exactly admit I was sitting at the kitchen table thinking about my novel on poverty. "I . . . uhh . . . was doing the dishes."

"You didn't get very far."

Baking cookies is a lot harder than it looks. Matt flips all the burnt cookies onto a rack to cool. Each one he inspects elicits a groan. "I guess we can eat some of these . . . but most of them . . . maybe Chelsea will eat them if I crumble them up and mix them with her grain."

"At least they won't go to waste."

"On the other hand, they may upset her stomach. Cows have a very delicate digestive system, you know. I'll take these ones out to the compost pile and bury them so the dog doesn't dig them up and get sick."

I flick the dish towel at Matt and scowl at him.

"You have enough for another batch. Try, try again!"

Matt darts out of the kitchen clutching a bag of ruined cookies. I spoon out more lumps of batter onto the cookie sheet and stick it in the oven. Just to be safe, I turn down the heat and then go back to the table to make a few notes.

Poor, Poor Rosie Brown—Plot notes

Rosie and her very large and very hungry family (she has eight younger brothers and sisters) get kicked out of their cramped and smelly apartment in New York City because they can't pay the rent. Their uncle Miguel has an old tug boat down in the harbour and Rosie's mother takes all the kids there and tells them to hide until she comes back.

Rosie's mother manages to get a job in a bakery which is really hard on Rosie because every morning, before dawn, she has to get up to look after all the kids. There's not nearly enough room on the tugboat for everyone and Miguel keeps dropping hints about how they should find somewhere else to stay.

I can't quite decide what to do with them after that. Something dramatic needs to happen or nobody will be interested in reading the whole book.

*One morning on the way to work, Rosie's mother gets
run over by a speeding fire truck and dies.*

That's pretty drastic, but it certainly is exciting.
Just as I'm getting ready to plan what Rosie will do
with all those kids and no money and an uncle whom
I think I'll make into a bit of a drunk, the oven buzzer
goes off and I nearly fall off my chair with shock. I
whip out the tray of cookies. No burnt edges this
time!

*Rosie tries to comfort the babies who are always
crying now that their mother is dead.*

"Those look better." Matt is back and picks up one
of the new cookies and takes a bite. Right away he
spits it out.

"What did you do this time? They're raw in the
middle!"

He pokes at the centre of the cookie. It's cold and
squidgy. He peers at the temperature dial. "Did you
turn that down?"

I sigh. There are some things I'm just not meant to
do. Baking cookies is one of them.

Matt stands there staring at the gooey cookie for a
minute. "Do you want me to make you a couple of
batches?" he offers.

"What will it cost me?"

"Five bucks."

"What!"

"I know you have five bucks in your account and
you are going to make more money tomorrow when
you sell these."

I can see my travel fund shrinking away before my
eyes. "Two dollars."

"Three."

"Two-fifty."

"Deal." He wastes no time. He clears all my feeble efforts out of the way and starts all over again.

"Do you mind?" he asks as he's whipping together butter and sugar. "I don't like to have an audience while I work. Especially you. You'll jinx the cookies."

"Fine." I stick my tongue out in his general direction, but I'm just as happy to retreat to Dove Cottage. During the time it takes me to finish outlining the plot of my novel, Matt bakes four batches of perfect cookies. He doesn't even use a cookbook. Somehow he just knows when the batter "feels" right. He makes enough for eight packages, each with six big chocolate chip cookies.

"How much are you charging for each package? I'll buy one from you." Dad is eyeing the baking hungrily. "I can't believe you didn't leave any out for us to eat."

I have no idea what the going rate is so I phone Alyssum.

"We charge a dollar for six cookies. Are you going to be ready to go at five-thirty?"

"What!! In the morning?"

"Of course in the morning. We have to get there early or we won't get a good spot."

"Five-thirty?" Quickly, I calculate how early I'll have to get up. "Five-thirty?"

"We'll be up way before that picking fresh produce from the garden. Do you want to come over and help?"

"No! I mean, not tomorrow—maybe another time?" Already I've decided this market stuff is just not for me. Getting up early makes me feel shaky all day.

"Meet us down by the end of the driveways—unless you have too much to carry. Then we could drive right up to your place to get you."

"No, no. The end of the driveway is fine," I say, looking at my little pile of cookies. "I don't have that much to bring."

"Great! We'll see you in the morning!"

"Who's coming, by the way? Will I get to meet the twins?"

"Oh, no. Not on market day. Mom will help pick the vegetables, but just Dad and I go to the market. When the twins are a little older, then they'll get to come, too. Unfortunately. They're such a pain. You can see for yourself tomorrow night. We get to come to your house for dinner."

Chapter Fifteen

Collected Quote #89
The perfect place for a writer is in the hideous roar of a city, with men making a new road under his window in competition with a barrel organ, and on the mat a man waiting for the rent.—Henry Vollman Morton
Source: Finding Time to Write Your Novel, 3rd Edition

By 5:45, when we pull into the park where the market happens, there's already tons of activity. Trucks, trailers, vans, cars, and even bicycles pulling carts are everywhere. People are putting up shelters, setting up tables, and unloading boxes, baskets, and bags full of every kind of fruit, vegetable, and homemade crafts you can imagine.

Alyssum and her dad, Morton, have a routine. They know exactly what to do. First they set up a brightly coloured awning that extends out of the side of their big, high-sided trailer. Three sets of table legs on three big tables snap into position. While Morton arranges the tables into a U-shape, Alyssum shakes out red and white checked tablecloths. Then, the most amazing procession of stuff begins to emerge from the trailer.

"Lyss, put the tomatoes in front at this end— they'll go fast!" Baskets full of lettuce, carrots, peas, potatoes, broccoli, cauliflower, and several strange-looking vegetables I've never seen before soon surround the tables. The tables themselves stay empty until all the produce is arranged for maximum effect.

"Put the spuds back here and move the leeks and onions up front—that's it, hang the garlic from the hooks."

Alyssum hardly needs to be told. She is arranging things as if she's been doing it all her life, which, I realize, she probably has.

"Time for the goodies," Morton grins, and Alyssum licks her lips.

Cinnamon buns drizzled with white icing, six different kinds of muffins, loaves of braided bread, some with tiny black poppy seeds sprinkled over the top and some shiny with glazed golden crusts, sugar cookies, iced cookies, lumpy-looking oatmeal-nut cookies . . . then, several cakes, pies with fancy lattice-work tops, and even two huge cheesecakes carefully set into a tray of ice.

"Wow!" I say, admiring the spread, but Alyssum and her dad ignore me and disappear into the back of the trailer again. When they come back, they are carrying a large turning rack filled with bottles and jars of spices, herb vinegars, and twinkling jars of jelly and jam—golden yellow, deep cherry red, and even something bright green—mint jelly.

Still they aren't finished! Soon a rack of candles and a basket full of handmade scented soaps squeeze onto the table behind a platter full of pinwheel cookies.

"Why don't you put your cookies over here?" Morton says, pushing two lemon loaves aside to make room.

"Ah, okay," I say, wondering who on earth will be bothered to buy my feeble offering of plain old chocolate chip cookies when there is so much other great stuff to choose from.

"Did you really make all this stuff?" I ask, astounded.

Alyssum nods. "Dad's specialty is the cheesecake. Mine is the soap. We all help with the baking and looking after the garden."

When the last bunch of cut flowers has been set out into a bucket of water, all I can do is stand back and admire the impressive display.

I have never seen anything like it. In the lettuce basket, there are at least four different kinds of lettuce. Alyssum is busy putting little signs out to identify everything. At least I'm not the only one who doesn't know the difference between a head of "Mignonette" lettuce and "Radicchio."

"What happens if you don't sell everything? You don't bring it back next week, do you?"

"The produce sells out first. We just about never take vegetables home. If we have leftover baked goods we take them to the Marigold Home for Seniors."

This is impressive. It reminds me of a fairy tale Granny told me about a poor girl who shares her last crust of bread with an old peddler woman. Somehow in the story this results in the girl getting a whole bunch of gold and a handsome prince. For Alyssum's sake, it's too bad things like that don't happen in real life.

All around us, maybe a hundred other people are doing exactly the same thing as Alyssum and her dad. By seven o'clock, everybody is ready, and by then the first customers have started to arrive.

"Why don't you have a look around before it gets too crazy," Morton suggests.

Alyssum and I disappear into the stalls and I think that even in Toronto I've never been to a place like the Tarragon Island Market. I only wish I had thought to bring my journal because before long there is so much going on I know there is no way I'm going to remember everything unless I write stuff down.

"Ah, this means *journey*."

The man with the stones has thick, short fingers. He's holding a smooth stone with a symbol painted on it that looks like a pointy capital letter *R*.

"Journey? Really?"

He turns the rune over and then holds it out towards me in his palm. "It can also mean 'life journey' or change, not necessarily that you will be going on a physical journey."

I nod, but I know which one it means. "Can I pick another one?"

He grins, showing a wide space between his two front teeth. "Only one freebie. I can do a Nine Rune Cast for you for only five dollars."

Five dollars. I'd love to know what else the fortune-telling stones can tell me, but I've already spent $2.50 paying for Matt's help with the cookies. The last time we checked back at the table, Alyssum's dad had only sold one package of my cookies.

"Not today. Maybe next week."

The stone man smiles at me and then waves at a woman wearing a deep purple, flowing robe. She looks like a gigantic grape. Grapewoman ripples and swoops over to stoneman and envelopes him in a huge hug.

"There's Tonya Windwoman." Alyssum points at a stand that looks like a Tiki hut. The walls are made of bamboo poles and the roof is made of thatched bundles of grass.

The paper lady's stand is divine. Everything on display is made out of paper that Tonya Windwoman has created herself.

"Hello, dear," she says, sweeping a long tendril of

black hair from her cheek. "I think I recognize you—were you in the paper?"

"The boat story."

"Ah, yes—how is the goose?"

"Barnaby? He's getting much better, thank you."

She nods and smiles. "So, you must be the writer. You just take your time and look at the special journals. No two are alike. In fact, no two pages are alike."

That's true. Embedded into every single page are petals, leaves, bits of what look like thread, and strands of something vaguely grassy. The pages are even different colours—from light blue to creamy yellow to pale, pale pink. The covers are something else.

Every book has its own design—leaves or ferns arching gracefully across the front cover, white petals arranged in a spiral against a blue background, even one journal with squiggles of gold and silver paint dancing across a sea of dark blue swirls.

"They're so beautiful."

"How about this one?"

Tonya Windwoman holds out a journal. The cover is made of copper that glows in the bright morning sun. The copper makes a kind of frame, not for a picture, but for a small mirror. I open the book and the pages are delicate, translucent.

"Rice paper," she says. "Imported from Japan."

"How much is this one?"

"Twenty-five dollars."

I put the copper journal back on the table with the others.

"Do you have a birthday coming up?" she asks kindly.

"At the end of the summer. On the second of September."

"The same weekend as the Wild Rose Festival! The

whole island will be celebrating with you." She pats the copper notebook. "You never know . . ."

"We have to go." Alyssum tugs at my arm. "You can come back later. We've left Dad alone for a long time."

During the time we've been gone, it seems like the entire population of Tarragon Island has arrived at the market. We have to push past children in strollers and ladies with big straw hats who carry bags laden with celery, fiery yellow plums, and loaves of fresh bread. Every other person seems to have a dog and all the dogs are intent on sniffing all the knees and feet that come within their reach. Everybody seems to know everybody else and nobody walks anywhere in a straight line.

"Jacob! Hi—how's the stone wall coming along?"

"Almost done! Do you still need help with the new well?"

A man with a baby on his back drops a bag of wooden toys right in front of me.

"Oh, sorry," he mumbles, and before the apology is even out of his mouth three or four people have stopped to help him pick up the trucks and cars and animals that have spilled everywhere.

"Hi, Byron. How's little Emily?" one man asks from where he is kneeling on the ground.

"Alyssum! Your dad's really busy. . . ."

"You're right—let's go!"

"Mandy!" a young woman shrieks and then throws her arms around another woman's neck. "I haven't seen you forever! How was Italy?"

It's so confusing I can hardly hear myself think. I step around the man with the baby and the scattered wooden toys, even more difficult to navigate now that his friends have stopped to say hello. The air thumps when drums begin to beat somewhere behind the "Organic Power Plants" stand.

"Uh-oh!" Alyssum breaks away from me and forces her way past a very tall, thin woman who is pushing her bike slowly past a stand of silver jewelry. Two tiny poodles perch in the oversized basket hanging from the handlebars. I can see why Alyssum is worried. The crowd is so thick around her dad and their stand that I can't see the tables.

When I push in closer, the whirl of activity dizzies me.

"Two pounds of potatoes today, Marion? Did you see the dill? Anything else? Alyssum! Great, you're back! Can you help Mrs. Wells?"

Alyssum is beside her father, scooping peas into a paper bag. "These go great with mint jelly, Mrs. Wells."

"Do you have any pumpkins yet, Mortie?"

"Not for another month, but they're looking good!"

"Hey, Morton, you available on the fifteenth? The first of my apples are ready!"

"Sure! Hey, did you get the truck fixed?"

All the while they are chatting to the customers, Alyssum and her dad are packing vegetables, wrapping cut flowers, handing over baking, collecting money, and making change. Just watching them work is like being at a circus or something, no two seconds alike.

"Can you give me a hand with this?" Alyssum asks, and I realize she's talking to me.

"Me?"

"Yes, you. Can you wrap up these soaps like this?"

I slip behind the table beside her. With smooth, experienced movements her small hands wrap each individual bar of soap in a piece of crinkly tissue paper.

"The lavender is new. I just made it this week."

A mother and her daughter are buying twelve bars. The girl has two long red braids and looks about my age. She keeps looking at me like I have three arms.

"This is Heather Blake. She lives next door to us. Her mom's the vet."

Alyssum can wrap three bars in the time it takes me to wrap one. The corners of my paper don't tuck in so neatly as hers.

"Ah, the vet's daughter—the one who survived the boating disaster! Pleased to meet you. My name is Henny Patten and this is my daughter, Emma."

"Hi." My thumbs keep getting in the way and I feel completely out of place.

"What grade are you going to be in?" Emma asks.

"Seven."

"Me too! We'll be in the same class."

"I guess so. What grade are you going into?" I ask Alyssum. There's a strange pause, like someone has turned down the volume at the market. Then Emma laughs.

"Alyssum doesn't go to school!" Emma says, as if I should have known.

I look at Alyssum beside me. She grins and concentrates on wrapping the last bar of soap. There's no chance for her to explain so I just stand there, feeling like a fool.

"Will that be everything for you, Mrs. Patten?"

"Yes, Alyssum. Thanks."

Alyssum takes the money and then darts off to the other side of the table.

"You should try some of these cookies. Heather made them."

Emma's eyes light up. "Chocolate chip!"

"Fine. I'll take a package of those, too. Alyssum, you are such a super salesperson . . . I never escape from your booth without all sorts of tasty extras."

Inside I'm just about dying with embarrassment. For one thing, maybe the cookies will taste awful, not at all like the gourmet baking from Alyssum's kitchen.

For another thing, I have the distinct impression Emma thinks I'm an idiot because I didn't know that Alyssum doesn't go to school.

I can't understand it. School is free, so it can't be money—unless her parents can't afford to buy her books or something. Then a horrible, sinking feeling churns unhappily in my stomach. Maybe there's something wrong with Alyssum. Maybe she has leukemia or something and she's going to die.

Watching her bounce happily from end to end of the stall chatting with all the customers, it doesn't seem very likely that she's on death's door. Then it occurs to me that maybe her mother is sick and Alyssum has to stay home and help raise the twins and keep the farm going with her dad, kind of like Rosie in my novel. I haven't ever met her mom. There must be a reason for that. Why doesn't she come down to get the mail instead of sending Alyssum? Maybe she's confined to her bed, tormented with pain and still responsible for those twins!

"Hey, Heather—can you carry Mrs. Gilbert's basket to her car?"

Mrs. Gilbert is bent nearly in half, she's so old. A huge hump on her back weighs her down so she can't stand up.

"Thank you, dear," she says when I pick up her heavy basket. She twists her head up at me and grins. She doesn't seem to have a single tooth left in her mouth and her gums are strangely mottled. The sight of her chases all my questions about Alyssum's health out of my mind. When finally, near the end of the afternoon, things slow down a bit, I take some of the proceeds from my cookie sales (everything sold, so I made eight dollars) and buy the smallest and cheapest notebook from Tonya Windwoman.

Chapter Sixteen

Collected Quote #100
I suppose I am a born novelist, for the things I imagine are more vital and vivid to me than the things I remember. —Ellen Glasgow
Source: <u>Mining Memories for Fiction Writers</u>, by Jacob Reiman

August 4th
I love writing in a new journal. And, this one is particularly special. I've never owned one with such beautiful paper. I found my fountain pen, the one Grandpa gave me last year for my birthday. The ink flows onto the page and I don't mean to boast but it seems like every word I write is more meaningful . . . more intelligent.

    <u>Saturday market notes</u> (jumbled because that's how the market is)

    -imagine a mob scene, strange people, first sighting of a kohlrabi (a kind of vegetable)

    -it was like being in a foreign country where I was the only person who didn't know everybody else, except most people spoke English

    -kites, tie-dye tablecloths, chutney, scented soaps, hand cream made from beeswax, a guy giving massages under a shady tree, two women and their babies dancing to the drummers, dogs everywhere including a gigantic golden dog that looked like a bear and knocked me on my butt when he stood up to lick my face

-made $8.00 selling cookies, spent five on a small notebook (this one I'm writing in), owe Matt $2.50 which means I only had $.50 left which was hardly worth depositing in my bank account so I bought some saltwater taffy from a lady called Pansy. Very sticky, but very good—sort of tangy and sweet.

I've been thinking a lot about my article on poverty. I think I might start it something like this:

The poor live haunted lives. You wake up in the morning and your tummy grumbles and you feel all light-headed, like you want to sink back into sleep. Getting dressed is a battle against shame—the same old rags day after day. Even washing your face is a chore when you have to go to the well to haul water.

Who could believe that in this day and age, in a country like Canada, there are families who go to bed hungry, waiting for welfare cheques that never arrive early enough?

Tarragon Island is no exception. The poor live among us, eking out meagre livings by selling vegetables at the market, though this means their own children are thin and scrawny.

There's lots more to write about but I have to go soon because Alyssum and her family are going to be here any minute and Mom said I have to help set the table.

I'm looking forward to seeing the whole Cranwell family together so I can see how being poor affects all of them. But I am sooooo tired. I wish I could just go to bed.

When the Cranwells arrive I can see my theory about Alyssum's mother being sick was completely wrong. Robust is a good word to describe her. She's taller than my dad and looks like a track star—and not just because she's wearing a tank top and very

117

short shorts. She has the most amazing muscles I have ever seen on a woman.

I suppose the twins probably have something to do with her fitness level. They are nine and a half months old and when you put them on the floor it's like letting go of two wild puppies. They crawl really fast and always in two different directions. When they reach something solid, like a table or chair, they grab hold and pull themselves up until they are standing. Then they start bobbing up and down on their stubby legs. Mrs. Cranwell chases after them with a cloth to wipe up wherever they dribble and drool, which is everywhere because they are both teething.

"Alyssum—can you play with the boys for a few minutes?"

"But I'm . . ." She's not doing anything, a fact that is clear to her mother.

"No buts. I need a break for a few minutes."

It's kind of embarrassing to watch someone else getting in trouble. I'd offer to do it, but I have no idea how a person is supposed to play with babies. Alyssum may not like entertaining her brothers, but she sure is good at it. She hides her face behind a cushion and then peeks out, making a rude noise with her tongue. Robert and Eric laugh and laugh with cute gurgling laughs. Listening to them I understand what people mean when they talk about chortles and chuckles.

"You try it," Alyssum says.

I take the cushion and poke my tongue out the way she did. Once I get the hang of it, her brothers laugh at me, too. Generally, I'm not a baby-loving person (way too much work!) but the twins are a lot of fun.

At dinner, I pay close attention to the grown-up conversation, hoping to get clues about why Alyssum doesn't go to school. Maybe she has a learning disability like Matt, but one that's so bad she can't go to a regular school at all. Matt needs extra help with reading and writing, but mostly he just does everything all the other kids do.

"Alyssum's very gifted in science," Morton says.

"I'm going to be a vet when I grow up."

My mom nods and swallows her spoonful of twelve-bean salad. After the clinic closed at three o'clock, she and Matt spent the afternoon in the kitchen preparing a whole slew of vegetarian foods. "In that case, science is very important. So is getting some hands-on experience, of course. You were excellent help in the clinic the other day. Any time you'd like to come over would be fine with me. . . . "

My mom looks at Alyssum and then at me. I know she wishes I were more interested in helping in the clinic. I guess she's forgotten how Alyssum fled when that scraped-up cat came in. It's not my place to remind her, so I keep my mouth shut.

"Alyssum is wonderful with the animals at our place. She has a real knack with the goats." Mr. Cranwell grins, like he's sharing a big joke with everyone.

"What kind of goats?" my mom asks.

"San Clemente goats."

My mom gasps and drops her fork. It clatters to the floor and Matt stifles a snicker. We're not used to seeing Mom throw her cutlery around. She's usually very big on manners.

"Really!? Did you know we just bought a Dexter cow?"

"I heard down at the market that Bill had sold one—I didn't realize it was to you!"

"Mom! They bought one of the Dexter cows!" Alyssum looks pretty excited, too.

Cows, goats . . . I cannot for the life of me understand how anybody could get so wound up about farm animals. Matt, though, has perked right up and jumps into the conversation.

"I saw San Clemente goats on the rare breeds list. They're endangered, right?"

"That's right! They're on the critical list. That means fewer than 2,000 in the whole world." Now Mrs. Cranwell is beaming. I feel like the only one at the table who doesn't know some secret password. I look over at my dad and he sort of shrugs at me without moving his shoulders.

"This is amazing!" my mother exclaims. "Who would have thought we would wind up with neighbours interested in rare breeds!"

"Incredible!" agrees Mr. Cranwell.

Then the conversation takes off at light speed with Matt, Mom, and all the Cranwells (including Alyssum) tripping over each other in their enthusiasm. I manage to figure out that both Dexter cattle and San Clemente goats really are endangered and that there are only a handful of people interested in breeding, raising, and protecting them.

"Oh, great idea, Morton! We could form an island society. . . ."

"To preserve and protect . . ."

"Rare breeds . . ."

"We're going to get a second Dexter cow. . . ."

"Hey, some of those dog runs could be converted into pens for chickens. . . ."

"Like Anconas?"

I can't believe how much Matt seems to know about rare breeds. His eyes shine as the grown-ups talk about the various kinds of old-fashioned farm animals they could raise.

"Brian Jennings down by the lake has Dominiques, doesn't he, Morton?" Alyssum's mother hands the twins to her husband and runs her hands through her short, blond hair. When she does that, her biceps bulge.

"Really? Mom, could we go see them, please? They're the coolest chickens! Could we get some chicks? I'll help look after them." Matt says.

"How about Barbados Blackbellies?" Alyssum's father stands by the kitchen window, swaying from side to side with a twin perched on each hip.

My mom nods. "Twenty acres is enough to raise some sheep."

"They're from Africa, aren't they? And they don't have wool."

At this, I have to interrupt. "Excuse me, Matt, but we *are* talking about sheep, aren't we?"

Then Alyssum pipes up. "Matt's right, actually. Some sheep don't have wool—they have hair."

Matt looks unbearably smug. He also seems a bit shocked, like he can't believe he can contribute so much to the conversation.

Alyssum's mother roams around the kitchen like someone with way too much energy to be inside. Somehow she reminds me of a leopard or a cheetah. "Come here, sweetie," she says and takes one of the twins (I can't tell them apart!) back. She sits down on one of the kitchen chairs and bounces the baby up and down on her knee until he giggles. "Rare breed preservation," she says seriously. "It's important work."

The two quietest people at the table are Dad and me. Dad makes a little signal to me with his eyes and clears his throat.

"If you'll excuse us for a few minutes, Heather and I have to check on . . . something."

Even though it's so obvious Dad just wants to leave the table, Mom doesn't seem to mind.

"Barbados Blackbellies. Are there any local

breeders?" she asks.

Dad and I head for the altar rock. It's big enough for both of us to sit side by side.

"Did you see the ad in the paper about the poetry reading at Wise Owl Books?"

To be honest, the only thing I read in the paper was my article. *That* I read seven times.

"Reading? Where will they put everyone?" Wise Owl Books is a tiny store in Rosehip, about a hundredth the size of the Old VB in Toronto. I haven't spent a lot of time there because first of all, we don't go to town that often, and second, it makes me sad and homesick because it reminds me of Charlie.

"Mitch and Bunny, the couple who own the bookshop, also own the tea shop next door. Apparently, that's where they have the readings."

I know that Dad wants me to say I'm dying to go to the reading and then he expects me to ask him to come with me, but what comes out of my mouth is quite different.

"Dad, why did you let Mom drag us here? Don't you miss Toronto?"

Dad pulls a long piece of grass from beside the rock and thoughtfully sucks on the end.

"A marriage is a partnership," he begins, and I'm almost sorry I asked. This sounds suspiciously like the start of a lecture and all I want to hear Dad say is that he wants to move back to the city as badly as I do.

"Your mother always wanted to have a mixed practice in the country. She's a farm girl through and through, you know. But in the beginning when I was establishing my career as an artist, I really needed to be close to the galleries and critics of Toronto and Montreal."

"So you gave up your career for her?"

"No. I still have a gallery in Toronto and my reputation is well established. I can paint anywhere and send my work to the buyers. So, we decided together that the time was right to give your mother a chance to fulfill her dreams."

"Pretty convenient that Poppa died when he did."

Beside me, Dad stiffens and holds his breath. Then he lets it out very slowly. I wonder if he's counting to ten in his head. I know it's kind of mean to talk about Poppa like that, even though it's true. Without the inheritance money Dad got from his father, my parents wouldn't have had enough to pay for the farm and all the renovations they needed to do when they built the clinic and a painting studio for Dad.

There isn't much he can say, I guess, and the silence goes on and on. I wonder if he's ever going to speak to me again and I get so worried he won't that I start getting desperate to think of something to say myself. That's the only reason I can think of that would make me blurt out the next question.

"So why did Auntie Pam get so much more money than you did?"

"How did you know that?"

"You and Mom talk louder than you think." I decide not to mention the part about the heating vent in the upstairs bathroom of the Toronto house. It feels like I'm about to get into trouble anyway and I don't want to make things worse.

Dad looks longingly back towards the house, like he's regretting his suggestion we go for a walk. But he doesn't get mad.

"You're growing up fast, Heather." He spits out a bit of grass and sighs. "Your mother told me you know about Adam."

I study his face, trying to figure out why he's talking about Adam when I asked him about Auntie Pam. She and her family live in England, not far from Nana. Now that I think about it, it's strange that Dad and Auntie Pam don't get along better. I mean, since his brother died, wouldn't he have tried extra hard to be friends with his sister?

"I only found out about Adam because you had a dream on the boat. You said his name."

"That was the same dream I've been having for nearly thirty years. In the dream Adam finds me, wherever I am, and he asks me to come sailing with him. And, just like the day of his accident, I say no because I already have plans to go to my friend Jack's house. Then Adam leaves. He sort of floats out of the house without saying goodbye. He drifts away and I run out of the house calling for him. But in the dream, I can't ever find him because he has gone sailing without me. On the boat, it was a little different. I thought I heard him up in the cockpit. I guess that's why I called out."

As Dad tells me about his dream his voice gets softer and softer until I can hardly hear him. A robin flits past us and lands not far away. We both watch as the bird tugs at a big worm and gulps it down.

"That must have been terrible." My words sound so small and useless. I want to lean sideways so my arm touches Dad's, but he's fiddling with another piece of tall grass like he doesn't know what to do next. He watches the robin who has hopped up onto a fence post. The bird looks back at us, tipping its head from side to side.

"Oh, Heather—you can't imagine how awful it was after Adam died. I know parents aren't supposed to have favourites, but in a lot of ways, Adam was a perfect son. He was everything I wasn't—good at school, a great athlete, good with people. Everybody loved Adam."

"Didn't Nana and Poppa pay extra attention to you and Auntie Pam after the accident?"

Dad's head tilts towards the sky and I look up and see a huge bald eagle soaring above us.

"You'd think that's the way it would have been. But no, for a lot of reasons, Poppa and I didn't get along. And since Poppa and I were always arguing, Nana also got upset with me. I know part of that was my fault . . . you know how you get when you decide you want to do something?"

I nod, guiltily thinking about how badly I want to run away.

"I suppose I should have thought more about Nana's and Poppa's feelings and how hard it must have been to lose their eldest son, but when I was a boy, what I wanted more than anything else was to have a sailboat. You can imagine Nana's reaction!"

I've only met Nana twice. She's very proper and doesn't like to get excited. I can't imagine my dad fighting with her, with anyone for that matter. Apparently, he did fight with his parents—worse, even, than I sometimes argue with Mom.

"If I'd had any sense, I wouldn't have harped on and on about not being allowed to sail. Now that I have children of my own, I know what a terrifying feeling it is to imagine something awful happening to you or Matt. I should have apologized, kept my thoughts to myself—but we never really made up.

"I moved to Canada to go to art school, married your mother, and started a family. Pam was the one who stayed behind, helped your grandparents look after the big house and garden. I suppose it makes sense that Poppa thought Auntie Pam deserved more money."

He sighs at the end of his long speech, like he's been saving up all his strength to talk to me. I feel grateful and grown-up that he feels he can trust me and talk to me like this. At the same time, Dad looks so sad, I want to change the subject—to anything that won't be so stressful.

"So, what are you painting now that we don't live in the city?" Dad's studio is usually out of bounds. Only Mom is sometimes allowed to see his works in progress, and then only when she's invited.

I have this idea that maybe we'll get back to talking about moving from Toronto since Dad always liked painting city scenes before. But when Dad gets up and starts walking towards the studio, I know I've completely lost control of the conversation.

Chapter Seventeen

Collected Quote #77
To write is to write is to write is to write ...—Gertrude Stein
Source: Charlie

I hesitate in the doorway of Dad's studio, uneasy about barging in. I've only been inside once, and that was on the first day, before Dad moved his stuff in.

The early evening sun floods through the windows and skylights, bathing the huge canvas on his easel so it looks like the light is coming from inside the painting.

Dad and I stand side by side in front of the picture. The first thing I notice is all the colours that Dad has put into the frantic water—not just blue like you'd expect, but green, white, brown, and gold.

Shooting up from inside the water is a boy who is being lifted by graceful white arcs that might be wings, or maybe sails. His hands cover his eyes as if he's too scared to look down.

Two jagged black lines cut across the whole thing, and make it look like the canvas is being ripped in half. White bubbles and froth swirl around the outside edges of the painting and make me feel like I'm being sucked down into a whirlpool.

"Sometimes," Dad says, "the most interesting

stories we artists have to tell are those we carry deep inside ourselves."

He squeezes my shoulder when he says that, like I'm supposed to understand what it means. "Never," he says gravely, "underestimate the complexity of the inner landscape."

It's a relief when I hear Mom calling from the house. "Ben? Heather? Dessert's ready!"

As Dad and I walk back down to the house, I reach over and take his hand, even though I'm really getting a bit old for that.

"Dad? Do you know who the poets will be at the reading?"

Dad smiles down at me like this is the best question I have asked him all day.

"I think Martin Thomas is the featured reader. He's coming over from Vancouver. And, I think there's also an open mic so local poets can read their work."

"Martin Thomas? Really? He's pretty famous! Charlie gave me one of his books—he could sign my copy!"

"Maybe you could take something of yours to read. . . ."

"Yeah—maybe I could finish the one I started about water being like glass and glass being like water."

His eyebrows push together in confusion.

"Never mind, it's a poet kind of thing."

He grins and gives me a friendly push into the house.

"Cheeky! Let's go see what's for dessert."

The discussion back at the dinner table has obviously continued non-stop while we were gone. My mom's animal books and rare breed magazines are strewn all over the table and everyone is poring over pictures of chickens that lay blue eggs, long-haired donkeys, and California Variegated Mutant Sheep.

"Shall we take the pie and coffee out onto the back deck?" Mom suggests.

"In that case, can I please go home and fetch the kids?" Alyssum jumps out of her chair, grinning.

"I don't know if that's okay with Bobbi and Ben. . . ."

"Sure!" My mom nods and winks at Alyssum's mother.

More kids? What the heck did I miss? Alyssum runs out the door without any explanation. The Cranwell family is weirder than I had imagined. Kids they don't talk about, wild twins, Alyssum not going to school. I hardly have a chance to mull it all over because in my head I'm trying to sort out what Dad meant when he said that stuff about the inner landscape.

Morton puts the twins down outside in the grass and waves his arms around to punctuate his points. Dad nods every now and then, though I don't think he knows much more about Khaki Campbell Ducks than I do. Which is nothing.

Sandy appears on the scene before Alyssum does. Mia spots her golden friend and flops over on her back. Sandy stomps on Mia's tummy with her huge paw but nobody has time to interfere because right then Alyssum bounds onto the deck followed closely by three baby goats.

Everyone freezes, even Mia, Sandy, and all three goats. From her upside-down vantage point, those goats must have looked pretty strange to Mia. She whines and a yip squeezes out of her before Mom springs into action. She scoops Mia up under her arm and laughs.

"These are your San Clemente babies?"

Mr. Cranwell nods but he doesn't have time to say anything because the goats have come unfrozen. They bounce around like they have rubber legs.

"Hey!" Matt giggles when one of the babies leaps up into his lap. It's about the size of a medium-sized dog.

"That's Mildred," Alyssum says. "And that one is Myrtle and there's Mabel. Mabel, no!"

Mabel is standing up on her hind legs reaching for the rest of the apple pie on the picnic table.

It doesn't take two minutes of the goats leaping over each other, scooting under the table, hopping up and down off our laps, before we are all laughing our heads off. Myrtle takes a flying leap, bounces off my lap and right into the middle of the picnic table!

"Catch her!" Morton shouts.

Myrtle is totally unconcerned with all the hoots and whoops of laughter and strolls quite nonchalantly over to the vase of flowers in the middle of the table and begins to munch on the nasturtiums.

"Maybe this wasn't such a good idea," Mrs. Cranwell gasps, looking like she is trying to rescue some dignity by clutching at her sides and breathing deeply. "I think we'd better take these naughty girls home! Thanks so much for dinner. . . ." Then she bursts out laughing again and it doesn't look like she's going to be able to go anywhere. This makes me laugh harder. Mom wipes her eyes with the back of her hand. I can't even hear a proper laughing noise from her any more—she's been reduced to making a wheezy, gasping sound and her face has turned bright red.

The only one who can move is Matt, who gently picks up the wayward kid and cuddles her to his chest. She slurps down the bright red flower hanging from her lips and then nibbles on his hair. He is still giggling when Mrs. Cranwell staggers out of her deck chair, catches two of the baby goats and strides down the deck stairs with one under each arm. Alyssum takes Myrtle from Matt and follows close behind her mother.

Still giggling, we all turn to look at Morton who has rounded up the twins and cradles them in his arms. Robert tries to pull on his father's ear and Eric stares intently at Mia who is wiggling in Mom's arms, trying to get free.

"Well," Morton says, blushing and sniffling. "Sorry about that. They can be a little rambunctious."

Eric squeals and squirms. "I think I'd better take these boys home to bed. It's been a long day. Thank you very much for dinner. Lovely to meet all of you properly. And thank you, Heather, for your help at the market today."

I nod, mutely. He sounds ridiculously formal after the crazy exuberance of his goats. His little goodbye speech gives us all a chance to regain our composure.

Mom, Dad, and Matt shout their final goodbyes and I feel like I've just been part of a very strange movie. Nobody brings goats over for dinner!

The rest of my family doesn't seem to think there's anything strange about our neighbours at all.

"What a lovely couple," my mom sighs. She ruffles my hair and smiles at me. "Isn't Alyssum a nice little girl? I was getting a bit worried you wouldn't have anybody close by to play with."

It bugs me that she doesn't consult me to see how I feel about Alyssum as a potential friend.

"We sure are lucky to have neighbors like that," my dad agrees.

"Can we really get some Ancona chickens?" Matt asks.

"May I please be excused?" I ask.

"Heather, are you okay?" Mom asks, but I don't feel like talking to her.

"I'm fine. But I'm tired. I was up early, remember?"

"Good girl for going to bed without being told."

She sounds so proud, like she did at the bank, so I decide not to tell her I hadn't planned on going to bed quite yet. I just want to get away from everybody.

"You're getting to be such a mature young woman," she adds, and then I really don't know what to say.

"Yeah, well anyway—good night."

"Good night, Heather," she says, and blows me a kiss. Dad winks at me and I leave them lounging on the deck and head up to my bedroom. As I climb the stairs, my arms and legs feel like they are filled with cement, and I realize that I really am tired. Even though I dig a book out of the boxes, I only make it through about two pages before my eyelids get so heavy I can't keep them open any longer.

The next morning before breakfast I decide to write my grandparents a letter.

Dear Granny and Grandpa,

How are you? I am fine. How do you like the special writing paper? I tore a piece from my new journal. I bought it at the Tarragon Island market.

I miss you a lot. I wish I could come to your farm and stay with you like I used to do in the summers. Granny, you won't believe this—I even miss your long fairy tales!

I figure I should give my grandparents some warning that I might be coming to Ontario so they have a chance to get used to the idea.

How do you like the newspaper clipping? I'm working on a novel right now and another story for the paper—both are about poverty, a subject I'm very interested in at the moment.

We have some really strange neighbours. They came over for dinner last night and they brought six kids!! Three humans and three goats! The goats were pretty cute, especially when one of them jumped on the table. I was laughing so hard I was crying and today my ribs hurt!

Dad says we are going to go in a sailboat race at the end of the summer. I don't really want to go in case we run aground or get lost or something, but I don't want to say anything to Dad because he's very excited about this race.

Anyway, I miss you lots and I'm making plans to come and see you sometime soon.

I scratch out the last part about coming to visit because I don't want them to tell Mom and Dad. I put a sticker over it in case they can read through my scribbles. It doesn't matter if they have any warning or not. I know my grandparents will be happy to see me when I finally get to their place, whenever that is.

The rest of the day is kind of lazy. Mom helps me sew up some proper curtains for Dove Cottage and then she sits in the cottage with me and we have lunch together. I like the way the curtains hang nice and straight and float in and out when the breeze blows.

The clinic is closed on Sundays, except for emergencies. Today Mom's beeper doesn't go off once and she seems like she's relaxed for just about the first time since we moved here.

"You know, I think we might have a couple of chairs you could have for visitors—so people don't have to sit on the floor."

I don't know how many people are going to visit me in Dove Cottage, but I appreciate her suggestion. She doesn't look too comfortable down on the floor. I offer her my desk chair, but instead she pats the blanket beside her and I move to sit on the ground.

Ever since the boating incident, she has been

really nice to me. I wonder how long this will last since I know the so-called disaster wasn't actually that much of a disaster and we weren't really in any danger of perishing at sea. It's not that she's normally mean to me or anything, but like she says, she works hard for a living and like anyone, she gets grumpy when she's tired.

Sometimes, when Mom and I are having one of our "rough spots" as she calls them, she says it's because we are too much alike. She says we're both stubborn people who hate to be wrong. Personally, I don't know anybody who likes to be wrong. Maybe she has a point.

After lunch, I help Mom sort out some more boxes for the kitchen—stuff we don't use a lot like wine glasses and the old mixer with the built-in bowl that turns around when you plug it in. The cupboards are getting pretty full so we have to move stuff around to make room for everything.

Twice I almost ask Mom if she knows why Alyssum doesn't go to school, but I don't want to spoil the nice mood by talking about the Cranwells. Instead, when I go back out to Dove Cottage by myself, I write a long list of questions about Alyssum in my journal. The school issue is Number One on the list.

On Monday morning, I make sure I'm at the mailbox early. I've decided to take the bull by the horns and find out for myself what the scoop is with Alyssum and her not going to school. She comes barrelling down the driveway at two minutes to ten. As usual, she looks down at something in her hand when she stops. This time, I can see what it is. A stopwatch.

"Forty-six seconds," she says, panting. "Not a

134

record. Mom says she's ready to start running again soon. I can't wait. Then I can really get in shape."

"Your mom runs?"

"She's an iron-woman."

"A what?"

"You know, those races where you have to run cross country and swim in the ocean and ride bikes and stuff? She's not a professional or anything. She just does it for fun sometimes."

"For fun?" Running marathons is not my idea of fun.

"Except when she's having babies, of course. Then she takes a year off. But now that the twins are bigger, she says she's ready to start running again. Then I'll have someone to train with."

"Train?"

"I'm going to run in marathons, too. Maybe if I'm good enough I can go to the Olympics. Here's the mail!"

We walk together to take the bundles from the mail lady.

"You want to come over?" she asks when Penny drives away.

"Sure." I try not to sound too eager, but I am more than ready to come and inspect her hovel. I've never been to a totally poor person's house before and it's really important that I get my descriptions right. I figure when we're inside I can pop the question about school. We jog down her long, curved driveway through the trees and then I stop dead in my tracks.

"Where's your house?" All I can see is a small hill rising in front of us.

"This is it."

She's not joking. The goats are tethered to the hill. One of them is tied to something that looks suspiciously like a chimney. A chimney sticking up out of the ground.

Sandy bounds towards us from around on the other side of the hill. She bumps me with her head over and over again until I kneel down to stroke her.

"We live in an underground house," Alyssum says. "It's very energy efficient."

"You live under there?"

She nods.

"How do you get inside?"

"Follow me."

We walk around the side of the hill and turn around. Now I can see how the house is built into the side of the hill. From the front, it looks like a house, quite a large house, in fact. Big windows face south over a brick patio.

"My room's over here on this side," Alyssum says, and leads me across the patio to a set of French doors. There are flowers and plants in big pots absolutely everywhere. She throws open the doors and we step into the most amazing room I have ever seen in my whole life.

Chapter Eighteen

Collected Quote #26
What we anticipate seldom occurs; what we least expected generally happens.
—Benjamin Disraeli, Earl of Beaconsfield
Source:Dad, when he tried to prepare me that I might not get exactly what I wanted for Christmas last year

"Stay outside, Sandy," Alyssum says, and closes the doors behind us.

Her bed is very high up, like a bunk bed. Instead of a second bed below, hers has a beautiful built-in desk and shelves underneath. A second, large desk stands beside a big window. That's where she keeps her computer. Two whole walls are filled with books, not novels like I have, but big books with titles like *Astronomy through the Ages*, *Earth Science in Canada*, and *The Ecology of the Great Bear Rain Forest*. Another shelf has a microscope, jars of paints, an abacus, and a complicated see-through model of a human skull.

There are posters on the ceiling of outer space, and posters on the walls of poor children carrying giant earthen pots on their heads. Models of all the planets in the solar system hang from her ceiling.

"That's my bathroom through there," she says, pointing at a door near the foot of the bed. "And that's the door to get to the rest of the house." The second door is blocked by a chest of drawers.

"This is all yours? You have your own bathroom?"

I want to scream, *There must be some mistake!* Alyssum has way more stuff than I do. More than anybody I have ever met. It's piled up all over the place, spilling out of shelves and storage boxes and strewn across the floor. I can't imagine how she ever finds anything.

Suddenly, I remember why I'm here in the first place. "Why don't you go to school?" It comes out more like a demand than a question. She answers me anyway.

"I home-school."

"Home-school?" I've never heard of such a thing.

"I study here at the house. Every fall I decide what I want to study for the coming year, and then Mom and Dad and I make a plan to figure out the best way for me to learn stuff."

"*You* decide what you want to learn?" That would never work for me. I'd decide never, ever to look at another number again. "What if you don't want to learn your multiplication tables? You mean your mom wouldn't make you?"

She gives me another one of her "you're not too bright" looks and shakes her head. "Of course not. There are some basic things we have to cover. But most of the time, I'm allowed to study what I want. Mostly I choose science and socials projects, stuff where I don't have to write much. I like making things."

She doesn't need to tell me. Drawings, leaf-rubbings, posters with pressed flowers, and handmade maps are tacked up all over the walls. There are lots of smaller models and projects around—a stick basket jammed onto the shelf by her bed, a miniature catapult made of Popsicle sticks on her desk, and wooden marionettes hanging from her bathroom doorknob. At least, I think they are marionettes—none of them have any heads.

"And all this is legal?"

Another look. "Of course it's legal. There are lots of families on the island who home-school. Sometimes we get together for special projects—like putting on plays and stuff."

Somehow, I cannot imagine not going to school and having my mother in charge of teaching me algebra. We would probably fight non-stop. On the other hand, it would be great to sleep in every day. . . .

"Some people think it's easier to home-school, but I don't think it is. We always have lessons right after chores in the morning and there's no way to hide it from my mom if my homework isn't done."

So much for my theory about sleeping in.

Directly under one of the skylights is a huge table covered with junk. It's such a mess, at first I can't tell what's going on. "Is this a home-school project?"

She nods. "I'm making a model of a village in Nepal. This part here is going to be a mountain."

The "mountain" is a cone-shaped blob made of papier mâché.

"This side kind of caved in. I have to fix it. Then I'm going to paint the whole thing grey." Alyssum points at an ice cream bucket overflowing with bits of moss, sticks, and pebbles. "Then I'm going to stick all these things on the mountain to make it look real."

"So, you're studying Nepal?"

"No. Water."

"Water?"

"Yeah. Like how people need water in their villages, and how pollution and stuff makes it hard to get clean water and how, if there's not enough water, people can't grow crops and they starve to death. I chose Nepal for my model village just because I like Nepal."

I don't know anything about Nepal, though when Alyssum lifts aside a pile of newspapers she's been shredding for the papier mâché I see a whole stack of books about the country. I suppose she'd let me read one if I asked.

"You could borrow this," Alyssum offers and hands me a *National Geographic* magazine with a river on the cover. "It has lots of good stuff about water."

"Maybe some other time." What kind of person could get excited about water? "Hey, how come you're working on this now—don't you get a summer holiday?"

A strange look passes over Alyssum's face—part guilty and part defensive. "Kind of. It's just I'm really good at starting projects and, well, not so good at finishing them."

That's when I notice several strange-looking things sticking out from the shelves under her high bed. She sees where I'm looking and then pulls one of the projects out for me to see.

"This was supposed to be a pyramid."

Several rows of large "bricks" form a square on a piece of board. Each layer is slightly indented from the one below it and I can see how it would eventually form a pyramid.

"I made the bricks out of soap—it's easy to carve and I thought I could make the stones look just like the ones in Egypt."

"It looks great! What happened? Why didn't you finish it?"

"One week I was short of soap at the market, so I wrapped up my next load of bricks and sold them. And then I got interested in spiders and made this web. . . ."

She rummages around in a drawer and pulls out a mess of sticks and coloured yarn. It doesn't look anything like a web.

"I don't know how spiders do it," she admits. "I tried five different ways and then I gave up. I drew a picture of one instead. It drives my mother crazy. She says I'm not allowed to start another project until I finish the water model. So, this year, school has kind of dragged on into the summer."

It must be awful not to be able to escape from school assignments, even on your summer vacation. I'm digesting this piece of information when she hops up and sits on the dresser standing in front of her bedroom door.

"Why do you have your door blocked off like that?"

"I don't want the twins in here. That's why we had to use the French doors. Now that the babies are mobile, they're dangerous!"

I can relate. I don't put furniture in front of my door, but I do hide my journal under my mattress so Matt doesn't read it.

"Mom makes me move it at night just in case there's a fire or an earthquake or something. But first thing every morning I push it back."

Even though I know we are underground, it doesn't feel like a cave or anything. Light pours in through the French doors and the two long, narrow skylights in the ceiling.

"Alyssum? Did I hear you come in?" A voice comes from a speaker on the wall. Alyssum presses a button on the intercom and answers her mother.

"Heather's here. She was down at the mailbox."

"Great! Hi, Heather."

I nod at the wall. "Hi." It's very strange to be talking to an intercom.

141

"When you two get hungry, I've just taken a loaf of banana bread out of the oven."

"Thanks, Mom."

Alyssum moves aside a mountain of rags, which I realize with a start is actually her clean laundry, and I plop into a comfy beanbag chair. Still disbelieving, I take in the music system, a video camera on another shelf, and a very large telescope.

"Before we have a snack, I want to check my stock portfolio. Do you mind? I haven't had a chance yet to decide where to invest my revenue from this week's market."

"Revenue?"

"I made nearly two hundred dollars. Dad and I were thinking it might be a good time to look for some new alternative energy companies. Do you invest in the stock market?"

I am so completely stunned I can't open my mouth. *Invest in the stock market?* People who invest in the stock market wear pinstriped suits and carry briefcases. They don't wear baggy tie-dyed dresses and running shoes. I'm not sure I even know what the stock market is!

As she works at her computer, Alyssum babbles on about ethical funds and supporting companies that build windmills and solar batteries. She mumbles about buying coffee from organic coffee collectives in Central America and profit-sharing with farmers. My head spins. It sounds like she's talking a different language. The more I gawk into space, the faster she talks.

"What's wrong? Don't you have a computer?"

"Yes. Sure. Well, my mom does and I get to use hers. We're still not hooked up to the Internet, though. We will be soon. I just . . . I just . . . the stock market?"

Alyssum doesn't answer, though she does look at me strangely. Hardly surprising since I can hear my

142

voice blathering on and know I'm not making much sense.

At the computer, she clicks and types and the monitor shows a page full of colourful graphs and charts. "These are some of my investments. This shows how the stocks are fluctuating in value . . . and this page over here lists good companies to invest in. Dad and I focus on businesses that are developing things like solar-powered cars and cheap medicines to be sold in developing countries. We go over all this stuff together and then try to learn all about each company before we decide whether or not to invest."

I sink deeper into the beanbag chair. Alyssum keeps clicking and pointing out stuff on her computer about international markets and being sensitive to the environment and water purification systems. She spins on her office chair and faces me.

"What did you say you were saving up for?"

My mind goes blank. I can't remember what I told her before. "If you must know, a bus ticket."

"A bus ticket? Where are you going?"

"Ontario."

"How much does that cost?"

"Seventy-five dollars."

"Do you have any money saved up yet?"

I think she's being very nosy, asking all these personal questions about money. I'm so stunned I can't think of a snappy answer, so I tell her the truth.

"Five dollars."

"Hmmm . . . I know you spent all the money you earned on Saturday. Do you need a loan?"

This is too much! "No! I mean, thank you, but no thank you. I'll figure out a way to earn enough."

She smiles. "Let me know if you need to borrow some. My interest rates are very competitive."

I don't want to hear any more about her stocks or

her money so I interrupt and ask, "Why did you ask me to help you at the market? I know I wasn't any help at all—I just got in the way."

Alyssum looks at me long and hard before she speaks.

"I felt sorry for you. You're new here and don't have any friends. I thought you might need some help getting to know people. It's hard when you move to someplace new. But mostly, I did it because my mother told me to."

"Because your mother told you to?!"

Alyssum turns bright pink. "Well, you just didn't look like a very interesting person. . . ." She looks shocked and then stumbles on. "I don't mean that exactly. I just thought that you would be boring since you are a writer. . . ." She shuts her mouth with a funny little popping noise and stops trying to explain.

I can't believe what I'm hearing! I struggle out of the beanbag chair. "I don't need your help to find friends! I don't care if I meet anybody on this stupid island because I'm not going to stay here!" She doesn't say a word when I storm out of her French doors and march around her fancy house in the ground.

The goats on the roof look up long enough to watch me head down the driveway and then go back to munching on the grass.

Chapter Nineteen

Collected Quote #44
A wastepaper basket is a writer's best friend.
—Isaac B. Singer
Source: It Was a Dark and Stormy Night; What Every Real
Writer Should Cut, by Alice Amore

When I get home I tear my poverty story into a zillion tiny pieces. The bucket I use for a garbage can in Dove Cottage is overflowing.

My pen rolls off the top of the overturned cardboard packing carton desk. I watch it disappear into the gap between the box and the old plank wall.

Who cares? I'll never be a real writer. Who am I kidding?

I kick over the bucket and bits of paper spill all over the place. I slump on the floor, my back against the wall. The pen pokes out from behind the box where it fell. I reach for my journal and start to write, my pen slashing heavy black marks across the clean page.

How dumb are you, Heather? The girl from the city who knows it all doesn't know a thing about the stock market, or home-schooling, or vegans. What makes you think you can write about poverty? What makes you think you can write about anything? You got the best marks in

Language Arts three years in a row but YOU DON'T KNOW ANYTHING!!!!!! And, on top of that, you are boring!

I hate to add that last part since I think Alyssum is the rudest person I have ever met in my entire life. Me, boring? She has some nerve calling me boring. She doesn't know the first thing about me!

I slam the book shut and pace back and forth until I stop in front of the pages of notes and the first two chapters of *Poor, Poor Rosie*. Poverty. *What do I know about poverty?* My hand reaches forward but something stops me from shredding the novel manuscript, too. Maybe one day I can salvage something. Maybe one day after I've done some real research with real poor people. Then, I might be able to write something decent.

My hands drop to my sides and my knees slowly buckle. I lie down on the blanket spread on the dirt floor like a carpet. Speckles of fine dust drift in the beams of sunlight sliding in through the old window. I squeeze my eyes shut and press the heels of my hands against my eyelids. Tears trickle past the barrier and I roll onto my stomach and cry and cry and cry, fistfuls of blanket clutched in my hands.

If only I could walk over to Maggie's place so we could sit on her porch and write in our journals and make friendship bracelets and drink hot chocolate. The more I think about Maggie, the harder I cry. She never thought I was boring!

A long time later, somebody knocks at the door. I'm tempted to stay down on the blanket and pretend I'm not here, but lying and hiding seem like too much effort.

"Heather? Are you in there?" It's Matt.

"What do you want?"

"Let me in. I need help."

I open the door, blinking in the bright sunshine outside.

"I suppose your new cow needs a bath?"

Jinnie, the new Dexter, joined Chelsea in the barn first thing this morning. Matt swears Chelsea is a happier bovine now that she has company.

"I'll give her a few days to settle in. Then we can bathe her. Jinnie's pregnant! What should we name the calf?"

"That's the fourth time you've told me that cow is pregnant. Is that why you're bothering me? To name a calf who won't be born until next spring?"

Matt looks like I've punched him and he almost turns and walks away before I can quickly say, "Okay. I understand why you've come to me. I know lots of great literary names."

He gives me a half smile. "Yeah. I guess so."

"Why don't we name it after one of the characters in *Charlie and the Chocolate Factory*?"

Matt really loves that book. He nods. "Yeah, he could be Charlie if it's a boy and . . ."

"Violet Beauregarde if it's a girl?"

He wrinkles his nose. "I don't like her."

"What about Josephine?"

"After Charlie's grandmother?"

"Sure. The Buckets are all nice people."

He squints up at a crow who has landed on the roof of Dove Cottage. "Okay. Charlie or Josephine. Thanks, Heather." He stomps back towards the barn, the pockets of his shorts bulging and the tops of his rubber boots making a thuckety thucket noise against his bare legs.

For a few days after my fight with Alyssum, the minutes crawl by so slowly I think I'll go completely crazy. I write letters to Granny and Grandpa, and

Maggie, and send off the kitchen poem to *Hot Stuff Poetry Magazine*. I can't bear to work on the Rosie novel and for some reason, no new ideas will come into my head. Dad has disappeared onto the boat again and if he's not actually avoiding me, he isn't exactly seeking me out, either. Mom, as always, is crazily busy.

It's actually a relief when Matt asks me to help him with his cows. He's practising every day, making them walk properly on the lead lines and then stop to look beautiful for the judge. I pretend to be the judge and look them over while he makes little squeaking noises with his lips to get their attention.

"It's so great Mrs. Cranwell knows about showing cows or I wouldn't have a clue what to practise!"

It turns out the Wild Rose Festival is *the* event to attend if you want to show off your livestock. The population sign when you get off the ferry says, "Tarragon Island: Pop. 4,782," and it seems like just about every family has a cow, or goats, or at least chickens. Apparently, lots of them come to the fair. Mrs. Cranwell says people come on the ferry from the other Gulf Islands and some farmers even make the trip from Vancouver Island. Matt is taking the competition very seriously!

No two cows have ever looked cleaner. He brushes them and gives them baths and buffs them up with a soft cloth until they practically glow. He even paints stuff on their feet to make their hooves glisten.

Everybody seems to be getting ready for something except me. Dad is always down at the boat, fiddling around with sails, the motor, the radio, his charts, the bilge pump, and the head, because he is still determined to go in the round-the-island boat race. Mom and the Cranwells keep phoning each other and having quick meetings about the future of the Rare Breed Rescue Centre. On Monday, they're going to start work fixing up some of the other farm buildings so there's room to put some of the new animals. By the sounds of it, between our two farms, we're going to have enough animals to start a zoo.

Judging by the way the Cranwells whip out their chequebook at the drop of a hat, they're so far from poor it isn't funny. I heard Mom tell Dad that the Cranwells made a fortune in real estate but even if they hadn't, it wouldn't have mattered because Mrs. Cranwell is the daughter of some rich guy who owns a bunch of grocery stores in the United States.

Even Barnaby is getting ready. He's getting stronger and stronger and soon Mom says she can take off the sling that's holding his wing tucked in close to his side so he can start exercising it properly. It won't be long after that before he can fly again.

I'm the only one who doesn't have a project. Okay, I do have a project, but one I can't do. Each time I try to call Mr. Turnbull down at the paper to tell him I can't write the story on poverty, I chicken out. Mostly, I sit inside Dove Cottage and feel time expanding around me.

Yesterday, things were so bad I spent fifteen minutes counting my heartbeat, seeing if I could change how fast my heart was beating by thinking about stressful things (like how on earth I could break the news to Mr. Turnbull that I'm a failure as a writer). It didn't work. I kept losing count and then I'd have to start again.

It's hard not to go down to the mailbox to meet up with Alyssum. She must think I'm a complete idiot, which, of course, I am. And rude. And selfish. And dumb, dumb, dumb. Of course, I'm not half as rude as she is. I keep reminding myself of that fact but it doesn't stop me from feeling lonely when a letter for me arrives from my grandfather.

Dear Heather,

Congratulations on your new career as a published author! Granny and I stuck your article on the fridge door and show it to all our friends when they come over.

Your neighbours do sound very interesting. They brought goats over for dinner? That's something your mother would have done when she still lived at home. She was always bringing sick animals into the kitchen to keep them warm. It sounds like your parents and Matt are very happy on Tarragon Island.

Your father has wanted a sailboat for many years. He must be learning a lot from his sailing experiences. I'm sure you'll all have a wonderful time in the boat race. There will be lots of people around if he should get into trouble again!

We miss you, too. You never know, we might see you sooner than you think. Here's a photo of us with Cocoa. Your grandmother insists on feeding that cat liver treats, and as you can see from the picture, his tummy is thanking her for her generosity!

I can't wait to read your novel—I've told everyone here that you are on your way to being Canada's next Marion Alsworthy. She's the one you met and liked so much, right?

Love,

Grandpa

P.S. Your grandmother says she will write soon, but I thought I'd pop this letter in the mail right away so you wouldn't have to wait too long.

I know reading Grandpa's letter should make me feel better, but it just makes me sadder. The only good part is the bit where he says he might see me soon. I guess that means he understands that I want to come and see them, but what he doesn't understand is how hard it is to earn and save money. When I write back to him, I don't say anything about coming to visit. All I need is to feel guilty about disappointing them when I don't show up.

The day I'm supposed to hand in my story on poverty creeps closer and closer. About a week before it's due, I screw up my courage and call Mr. Turnbull.

"Hi there, this is Heather Blake."

"Hello, Heather! How's the story coming along?"

"Well, I wanted to ask you something about that. . . ."

"What a coincidence! I was going to call you about your story!"

A sigh of relief escapes from deep inside me. He's going to cancel the story so I don't have to tell him I can't do it.

"The paper that comes out the week of the Wild Rose Festival is always really full. Would you mind holding off and submitting the article the week after the festival is over? I hope you're not too disappointed that it won't run earlier. . . ."

"Errr . . . no, of course not. The week after the festival would be fine."

"Great! Now, what were you going to ask me?"

"Um . . . actually, nothing. I was just, um, checking to see if you still wanted it because we haven't talked in a while and—"

He interrupts and booms into the phone so loudly I have to hold the receiver away from my ear. "Of course I still want it! I've had great feedback about your last story. I'm thinking about starting a regular column written by talented young people like yourself."

"Oh. Gee. Great!" I hope I sound more enthusiastic than I feel. When I hang up the phone, instead of feeling relieved, I feel even more desperate than before. If I hadn't called and had just "forgotten" to hand in the story, maybe Mr. Turnbull would have forgotten that he had ever agreed to look at another one of my articles.

Now that I've called him and refreshed his memory, I simply have to come up with a story. No two ways about it, I'm stuck, stuck, stuck. When I get really stuck, I have a way of coping. I procrastinate. The week after the festival will be plenty early to seriously worry about the dumb article. In the meantime, I decide to push it out of my mind and pretend like I'm not going to be completely humiliated in front of the whole population of Tarragon Island.

Chapter Twenty

Collected Quote #10
Any writer worth the name is always getting into one
thing or getting out of another thing.—Fannie Hurst
Source: Mrs. Thompson, Grade Five teacher after she
caught me spying on the Grade Sevens to get accurate
details about how teenagers talk

Just when I'm beginning to think I'll spend the rest of
my life stuck staring at the dust particles suspended
in the warm August air of Dove Cottage, time speeds
up like someone has turned the world onto fast
forward. With the Wild Rose Festival only three days
away, there's so much to do I hardly have a minute to
myself.

Dad is in overdrive, polishing up the boat and
making sure he has all the safety equipment he might
possibly need stowed away safely on board. We head
down to the boat right after breakfast on Wednesday.

"How many cans of peaches?" Dad's preparing an
inventory of all the food, water, and other supplies on
board *Ariel*.

"Fourteen."

"Tins of tuna fish?"

"Six."

"Salmon?"

"Four."

"Pancake mix?"

"Two large boxes."

"Check the seals on the plastic containers."

I check to make sure the lids are on tightly. The containers are supposed to keep the pancake mix from getting mouldy on the damp boat.

"Check."

"Cooking fuel?"

"Check."

"What do you think Alyssum would like for lunch on race day?"

My mouth gets dry and I feel my heart flip-flop behind my ribs. I've been avoiding Alyssum ever since the day I went to her house and made a fool of myself and she insulted me.

"Alyssum?"

"She didn't tell you?"

"Tell me what?"

"She signed on as a crew member for the race."

"She did? On *this* boat?"

"Well, actually, I signed her up. We're a bit short of capable crew."

Horrified doesn't describe how I feel. *Ariel* is not a large sailboat. There is no way to hide from Alyssum for a whole day.

"Morton says she's an excellent sailor. We can use all the help we can get."

Wild excuses fly through my mind. Maybe I could get sick, have a migraine headache or something. They are supposed to be horrible—debilitating, according to Granny who gets them occasionally. Maybe I could get food poisoning, or a fever, or fall and twist my ankle. Then I wouldn't have to go on the boat at all.

"Hot chocolate powder?"

"One canister."

"Sugar? Coffee? Tea?"

"Check. Check. Check."

Dad keeps reading from his list and making neat little tick marks beside each item. Then he writes down the locker or drawer number where everything is stored. There's so much food on board, we could have fifteen people stranded at Billy's Cove for a week and nobody would go hungry.

At lunch, we sit in the cockpit and unwrap our sandwiches.

"How are you doing with your poverty article?" Dad asks.

"I hate writing." I know it sounds melodramatic, but it's how I feel. I don't think I'll ever be able to write anything again. "Don't you ever get stuck with your paintings?"

Dad munches thoughtfully on a carrot stick.

"Yes and no. Sometimes it's very frustrating when what I see in my head doesn't look right on the canvas. But then I remind myself how hard I fought for the right to be a painter."

This is news to me. "I thought you always liked to draw, even when you were a kid."

"Sure—I loved to draw the same way you love to write. My love for art was another thing I fought about with my parents. They didn't believe that being an artist was a real profession. They wanted me to be a doctor or a lawyer, or at least a banker like Poppa."

"Like Adam was going to be a doctor? Uncle Adam."

Across the bay, the water ripples, making the reflections of the sailboat masts jiggle up and down.

Dad nods, takes another bite of sandwich, and chews very slowly before he goes on.

"After Adam drowned, my sister tried very hard to fill the gap he left behind. I did, too, in my own way—though Nana and Poppa never saw it like that! Auntie Pam studied and studied, which is how she wound up teaching physics at university. But me, well, I couldn't stop drawing even though I actually tried for a while. When I started painting again, it didn't help matters that my favourite subject was sailboats."

I sit very still, not chewing my sandwich, not wanting to interrupt, hoping Dad will tell me more.

"Until the day he died, my father believed I made the wrong decision, that I wasted my life by being a painter. He was a stubborn old man—and, I suppose I should thank him for passing on the 'stubborn' gene because that's what makes me sit down in front of my easel, day after day, until finally, I paint the pictures I want to."

He turns his head away before he continues.

"You know, I see the same trait in you. Which is why I'm sure you'll get back to work and write another fine story. Many fine stories."

I wish I could say that I find his words encouraging. But actually, they're heavy and weigh me down with a kind of responsibility I don't want.

"Well, matey—how about we swab the decks?"

For the rest of the day we scrub and polish and organize until everything aboard *Ariel* is shipshape.

I wish I felt as good as that boat looks. But when we climb on our bicycles and ride home together, the quiet between us seems filled with sadness, and neither Dad nor I can find the words to lift our spirits.

Chapter Twenty-one

Collected Quote #67
Writing is one of the few professions left where you take all the responsibility for what you do.—Erica Jong
Source: Inspirational Quotes for Writers, 4th Edition

Matt plans to spend the whole day on Friday getting Jinnie and Chelsea beautified for their classes the next day at the agricultural fair.

"But, Mom! I want to go and watch the parade."

"Sorry, Heather. You have to help your brother with the girls. I can't do it because I have two surgeries booked for this morning, and your father is putting the finishing touches on a painting he has to ship to Toronto next week."

She puts her hands on her hips and sets her chin. Then her face softens a little and I can see how tired she looks.

"Okay. I'll help."

"Thanks, Heather." She smiles and gives me a quick kiss on the forehead.

In truth, I don't really care if I miss the parade. I'm pretty sure Alyssum and her family will be there and I don't want to run into her. But that doesn't mean I want to help Matt wash his silly cows *again*.

With both cows going to the fair, he has a thousand things to do to get them both ready.

Chelsea will be competing against other young heifers, but Jinnie is old enough to compete against more mature cows.

"Won't she lose points because she's pregnant?"

"Of course not. Cows are supposed to get pregnant or they stop giving milk."

This sounds like a basic fact of life I should have known so I lie and say, "I knew that."

The "girls" have become very tame. They actually seem to recognize Matt when he slips into their paddock. Chelsea in particular is very curious, especially when it comes to figuring out which of his various pockets contains the grain.

When, finally, he has finished combing the little tufts of hair at the ends of their black tails, and cleaned and oiled their halters, we put the cows into the barn for the night, ready to be hauled to the Agricultural Centre at the crack of dawn tomorrow.

I don't know what it is about farm animals, but they don't seem to need a lot of sleep. Chelsea and Jinnie are both wide awake when Matt and I stumble out to the barn to wake them up at 4:30 in the morning.

"Why do we have to get there so early?"

"Stop whining," Matt says, doing a perfect imitation of Mom's scolding voice. "Judging starts at eight sharp. We need time to touch them up when we get there."

The cows look perfect to me. Once Matt has whisked over their soft, black coats with a stiff brush, not a single wisp of straw or dust is left on them anywhere. Dad backs the truck up to the barn and lowers the loading ramp to the ground.

"Good thing they're small cows," he says, as Matt leads first Chelsea and then Jinnie up into the back of the pickup truck. Our truck has been transformed into a cattle-hauling vehicle with the addition of wooden sides that Morton and Dad built on the back. Tempted with handfuls of grain and Matt's constant reassuring words, the girls load quickly and easily. Mom helps Matt tie the heifers securely. She gives him a big hug and tells Dad to take lots of pictures.

"I sure wish I could be there to see you."

Before I know it, we're on our way, leaving Mom standing in the driveway, waving.

Schedule of Events:
Tarragon Island Wild Rose Festival

Friday
9 am—Parade
11 am - 6 pm—Music Festival

Saturday—All day
Livestock Fair—Agricultural Centre
Pet Show
Blindfold Rowboat Races
Recycled Boat Building Contest
Pie-Eating Contest
Marketplace
Flower Show
7 pm—Tarragon Island Players—Play:
"The Island Menace"

Sunday—All day
Round the Island Boat Race
Tarragon Island Fall Horse and Pony Show
6 pm—Salmon Barbecue

The grounds of the Agricultural Centre are crawling with people and their animals, even though we arrive just as it's beginning to get light. Dad helps unload and then gives Matt a big hug. "Good luck, son."

"Where are you going?"

"I have to run over to Victoria on the first ferry to pick something up. I'll be back later this morning."

Matt bites his bottom lip. "But you'll miss my class!"

Dad winks. "I'll be back in plenty of time for the championship classes this afternoon. Heather will give you a hand, won't you?"

I nod. What choice do I have?

"What does he have to get in Victoria?" I ask as we watch the truck bump away over the grassy field behind the Agricultural Centre.

Matt shrugs. "Something for the boat race, I guess."

"Another new radio, maybe?" We laugh and then turn and walk together towards the livestock sheds. Any thoughts of what Dad might be picking up over on Vancouver Island are pushed aside when we are caught up in the excitement and tension of the other competitors, all grooming, polishing, and buffing up their prize animals.

Matt flies into a mild panic when he sees that Chelsea's lips are green and frothy after her breakfast of fresh hay.

"Where's the washcloth?"

I root through the duffle bag filled with cow grooming equipment and hand him one of several clean cloths he has packed just for this purpose.

"Water! I need a bucket of water!"

"Calm down, Matt. I'll find you some water."

A man who is grooming his llama directs me to a faucet and I fill our bucket. Matt dips the cloth in the clean water and carefully wipes his cow's lips. She hardly notices and just keeps on chewing her cud, her look of contentment a stark contrast to Matt's nervous excitement.

After a final flurry of brushing and polishing, Matt leads Chelsea into her class. I find a spot near the entry gate so I can watch. It's amazing how nervous I am, how exciting it is to watch a bunch of heifers walk around in circles.

As the judge carefully considers the entries, my hands ache from gripping the top rail of the fence, and when Chelsea wins a first in her class, I let out a whoop and slap Matt between the shoulder blades when he comes out of the ring.

A short time later, we go through the whole routine again when Jinnie comes second in her class against several spotless cows, all of which are considerably larger than our Dexter. Matt positively beams when he leaves the ring holding tightly to Jinnie's lead rope.

"Wasn't she great? Did you see how she looked the judge in the eye?"

Matt is beside himself with excitement. "They're both in the championship class, Heather! Both the girls made it! First and second place cows from all the different classes get to go on!"

He turns and kisses Jinnie on the nose. "Matt! Don't kiss your cow in public!"

A look of horror passes over his face and for a moment I think he has come to his senses. Then I realize his concern has nothing to do with kissing cows in a public place.

"Heather . . . how can I handle both of them in one class?"

This is a good point. The rule is one cow per handler.

"Heather, you'll have to take Chelsea. She's calmer. You don't know what you're doing and Jinnie needs my support."

"Hang on a minute—"

"We don't have a choice! Otherwise I can only take one of them into the championship class!"

"I'm only here to help you get them ready. I don't know what to do!"

The thought of standing in front of a judge and audience holding a cow does not appeal to me at all.

"Heather, please. You have to help me . . . Dad might not be back in time. . . ." His face crumples.

"Don't cry. Mattie, please don't cry. Fine. Fine. I'll do it."

Matt looks hugely relieved and wipes his nose on the back of his sleeve. "We'd better go practise. I'll show you exactly what to do."

Matt and I wolf down hot dogs for lunch. We try to look around at all the animals and displays of produce, baking, flowers, and handicrafts, but Matt is such a nervous wreck it's impossible to relax and look at anything properly.

"Where's Dad?" he asks when we're lining up outside the show ring, waiting to go in for the championship class.

"How should I know, Matt. He probably got lost finding the ferry terminal."

Our father is famous for his ability to get lost.

"He'll be here, don't worry. You don't think he'd miss your moment of glory, do you?"

Matt shrugs. His shoulders are thin and stooped. "Stand up straight, Mattie. You have to walk into that ring looking like a winner or you'll never get anywhere."

He smiles weakly and straightens up. The stress is getting to him, I can tell. His hands are shaking when he coils and re-coils the lead rope.

"Remember to make that little noise when the judge comes past to inspect Chelsea," he instructs for the hundredth time.

"I know, I know. We'll be fine. You just concentrate on Jinnie."

And then, we're in the ring, leading the cows around the outside of the ring so the judge can see how they move before we line up.

It's right when I'm leading Chelsea past the

viewing stands that I have my most alarming hallucination yet. I look up into the stands and I swear I see Granny and Grandpa sitting there right beside Dad. The hallucinations wave and smile at me. Granny takes off her big straw hat and waves that for emphasis.

I swallow hard and look away, trying not to cry. If only they *were* here, then everything would be okay. For the whole rest of the class I concentrate on Chelsea and doing everything exactly as Matt has told me. I don't dare look back up at the stands because I don't trust myself not to burst into tears. Instead, I lift my chin and try to imagine that I am holding the lead rope of a grand champion cow.

It seems to take forever for the judge to choose the best cow of the show. There are twelve finalists who have qualified in earlier classes. Finally, the announcer's voice crackles through the loudspeakers.

"The Reserve Champion for the Twenty-ninth Annual Wild Rose Festival is Glorious Bluebell, a truly glorious Guernsey cow. And the winner, our Grand Champion Cow, is Chelsea, a Dexter heifer owned by Matthew Blake and handled in the ring today by his sister, Heather Blake."

I step forward to shake the judge's hand while the ring steward fastens a huge, fluttering blue and white ribbon to Chelsea's halter. Out of the corner of my eye, I can see Matt standing close by with Jinnie. His grin just keeps getting bigger. He looks like he wants to say something, but no words come out. He just breathes faster and shakes his head.

I gesture to the ring steward to hold Chelsea. Then I run over to Matt and grab Jinnie's lead rope.

"What are you—?"

"Hurry! Go claim your ribbon!"

Matt rushes to Chelsea and right in front of the surprised steward, kisses his cow on the nose. He takes the fluttering ribbon from Chelsea's halter and waves it above his head. Then he leads the procession of cows from the ring. Jinnie and I jog to catch up to him.

"Mattie! Heather!"

I stop in my tracks, not daring to believe what I think I'm hearing.

"Heather!"

Slowly, I turn around and I'm swallowed up by Grandpa's huge, warm hug. He smells just like I remember, a mix of peppermint and freshly cut grass. "Grandpa!"

When we untangle ourselves, Granny rushes over from where she has been hugging Matt and I throw my arms around her neck.

"I thought you were a hallucination!"

Granny laughs. "I should hope not! But you can pinch me to make sure!"

We both laugh and I give her arm a gentle tweak. She is as real as real can be.

"This is what you had to pick up in Victoria?"

Dad nods. "I nearly missed the turnoff to the airport. And then, coming back the ferry was nearly full. We were lucky to get here in time for the championship!"

Dad's mention of the championship brings on a fresh round of congratulations and Grandpa slaps Matt on the back so hard he nearly tips right over.

Chapter Twenty-two

Collected Quote #124
If at first you don't succeed, try, try again.
Source: Granny

"So then we went to the strawberry pie tasting tent and Grandpa ate two whole pieces of strawberry pie!"

"With ice cream," I add. I had almost forgotten how much Grandpa loves to eat! Despite the fact he sampled cookies, pie, fresh bread, corn on the cob, and a huge sausage with sauerkraut at the fair, he is still vigorously attacking the chicken and baked potato on his dinner plate.

"Ah, Bobbi—I've sure missed having dinner with you and the kids."

Granny nods. "I'm so glad I managed to convince your father to come out here for a visit."

"Well, you don't think I'd miss my Heather's birthday, do you? Is it your tenth? Eleventh? Naw, couldn't be."

I laugh at Grandpa's joking. "Thirteenth, Grandpa. I'll be thirteen tomorrow."

He shakes his head, leans back in his chair, and strokes the sides of his round belly with a sigh of deep satisfaction.

"So, Heather, you're spending your birthday on a sailboat, hmmm?"

"Hey, Grandpa—you like boats, right?"

I know very well he does. When I used to go over to my grandparents' farm in the summer, he would read chapters of *Swallows and Amazons* to me and he'd always get all excited when the kids cast off from shore and sailed out into the lake.

"Well, you know I like the idea of sailing. But like your dad, there, I haven't had a whole lot of experience."

"I could call Alyssum and tell her that since we have unexpected guests, there's no room for her. Grandpa can take her place. I'm sure she'll understand."

I feel very smug. Nobody needs to know that Alyssum is no longer my friend. And if I have Grandpa along on the boat, maybe I can find a few quiet moments to talk to him about taking me back to Ontario when they leave.

"That won't be necessary. There's plenty of room for all of us. Besides, Alyssum is the only one with any real experience. She's also done the course before so if she comes along we're less likely to get lost!"

I know Dad has been studying every millimetre of the trip on his charts and the weather forecast is for sunshine in the morning, but I don't say anything else. There's no point. Dad has obviously thought everything through.

"The more the merrier, that's what I say," Grandpa says, beaming. "I'd like to meet this friend of yours, Alyssum is it?"

"You don't have to wait long—we've got an early start tomorrow!"

Just the mention of getting up early again suddenly reminds me how completely exhausted I am. Mom must see me sagging into my chair because right then she says, "Heather, Matt, Dad—if you want to be useful in tomorrow's race, may I suggest an early night?"

Even though it's not even dark yet, I nod wearily and plod upstairs to my bedroom. I don't even have the strength to plan what I'm going to say to Grandpa the next day on the boat. "The more the merrier," I mumble to myself, half asleep. I sure hope that's how things turn out.

"Wow!"

Grandpa sighs in awe at the view as we come around Tarragon Point at the south end of the island. We've only been underway for about an hour and I think he has said "Wow!" about a hundred and fifty times.

Ariel's crew is finally beginning to work like a team. Alyssum is beside Dad at the helm. Even though he is the one shouting out the directions to the rest of us, Alyssum is the one who tells him when it's time to tack and suggests the direction we head. I see her nudge my father and then he yells,

"Ready to come about?"

I brace myself up on the foredeck. It's my job to make sure the front sail, the jib, slides smoothly across the boat in front of the mast when *Ariel* turns.

"Ready!" I yell back, loudly so he can hear me in the wind.

"Ready!" shout Alyssum, Grandpa, and Matt in the cockpit.

"Coming about!" Dad yells and leans hard on the tiller. There's a rush of activity as Alyssum whips the sheet off the winch when the boat begins to turn. With a whizzzzz, the soft rope slithers along the deck. The jib flutters wildly when the sheet goes slack and then begins to fill again as *Ariel*'s nose falls away from the wind.

"Go, Heather!" Matt screams in excitement as I flip the edge of the sail clear. I hang onto the mast with one hand and then turn and wave with the other. In the cockpit, everyone ducks as the heavy boom swings over their heads. Then Grandpa pulls in the slack of the sheet that he's wrapped snugly around the winch on his side of the boat, and Matt tugs at the end of the rope to make sure everything is tight.

"That was the best one yet!" Dad shouts, and sticks his thumb up. The members of the cockpit crew cheer so loudly you'd think they'd won the whole race and not just managed a tidy tack!

Up on the foredeck, I lean up against the mast and close my eyes. I'm getting used to the way the boat heels over when she scoots across the water. The day is perfect for sailing—a stiff breeze, a light chop on the water, and brilliant sunshine lighting up the colourful sails of all the other boats in the race. The leaders have already passed Storm Island and disappeared from our sight. Obviously, we aren't going to win this race. But here and there all over the channel between Tarragon and Verona Islands, smaller boats like ours scud along, tacking back and forth before the wind, their crews laughing and cheering and waving wildly when we pass each other.

So far, Alyssum has completely ignored me, which is fine since I'm completely ignoring her, too.

About halfway through the race, Matt crawls forward to join me on the foredeck.

"Hi. Dad sent me up with a sandwich."

"Thanks, I'm starving!"

"You're lucky. It's way more fun up here! I wish I didn't have to stay in the cockpit. Alyssum's bossy."

"Maybe next year you can do this job." Normally I would have offered to switch for a while, but it

168

would be impossible to avoid *her* in the cockpit. "Yeah, she's a bit of a know-it-all, isn't she?"

Matt nods and looks rather unhappy.

"Ready to come about?" Dad yells from the cockpit.

"Oh no!" I say. "What about my sandwich?" I stuff it down inside my life jacket and hope it doesn't get too squished before I have a chance to eat.

"You'd better get back there," I say, nudging Matt in the ribs. "He sounds a bit panicky!"

"He's getting the hang of it. She's bossy, but I guess Alyssum's a good teacher." He looks at me for a minute like he's going to say something else.

"Go!" I say. "Hurry—Dad's going to tack." Matt scrambles back toward the cockpit and I get ready for another change in direction.

"So then, we cleared the point up at the north end of the island and the wind stopped!"

Grandpa is giving Mom and Grandma a minute by minute replay of the entire sailboat race over dinner. The Cranwells (including the twins but not the goats!) have come over for a barbecue to celebrate the fact that not only did *Ariel*'s crew survive intact, we didn't even come in last. In fact, we came in twenty-seventh out of thirty-five boats. Dad is ecstatic.

"To my crew!" he says, beaming at everyone. We all raise our glasses of punch and cheer.

Grandpa is just getting to the part where we nearly ran aground at Taylor's Rock, when Mom comes up behind me, singing.

"Happy Birthday to you, Happy Birthday to you!"

Then everyone is singing, including Sandy who starts howling like a lone wolf. That gets Mia going and Grandpa says, "I'd say this party is going to the dogs!"

I cut pieces of cake for everyone. When I've finished licking the last crumbs of chocolate from my plate, Mom gives me a meaningful poke and says, "Heather, why don't you show Alyssum your room?"

Dad is suddenly intent on scraping every last crumb from his plate. He must have reported to Mom that I didn't say a single word to Alyssum all day.

"That's a good idea, Alyssum," Mrs. Cranwell says pointedly.

Obviously, there's a conspiracy going on among all the parents because then Morton says, "Maybe you could ask Heather for some help with your new project?"

The way Alyssum glowers at him I know she isn't any more interested than I am about having to socialize up in my room.

I grind my chair backwards across the floor and stomp out of the room.

Grandpa launches into yet another replay of *Ariel*'s dash for the finish line and I hear my mother say, "Heather's room is at the top of the stairs."

When I get to my room, I sit on a box near the window. I'm determined not to even look at Alyssum. I can hear her come into the room behind me and then my bed squeaks.

The silence goes on and on and I have to fight the most bizarre urge to laugh, even though there isn't anything remotely funny about this situation. Outside, I can see Mathilde stalking something through the tall grass.

"Lots of boxes," Alyssum says. It's a huge relief when she finally says something. I turn around and see she is surveying the clutter.

"When are you going to unpack?"

I shrug. "Maybe never." I restrain myself when she peers into an open box. Mom would kill me if I beat up my guest. But really, she is so nosy it's all I can do not to say anything.

"What's this?"

She fishes a plaque out of an open box by my bed.

"Nothing. A prize I won at school for an essay contest."

"That's not nothing," she says firmly. "You're so lucky. I hate writing, but my mom says I'll never be a good scientist if I can't write down my ideas."

"I'd say you'll never be a good scientist if you can't finish any projects."

She carefully props my plaque up on the empty shelf by the head of my bed and flops back onto the pillow with a huge, shuddering sigh. She looks so small and miserable I'm suddenly swamped with guilt.

"I'm sorry," we both blurt out at the same time.

There's another long silence and then Alyssum says, "I don't really think you're boring. I just thought you were *going to be* boring. Now that I know you a little, I know you're kind of mean."

"What!?" She's right, of course, even though I can tell by her little smile that she's not seriously trying to pick another fight.

Still, I don't want to say anything that she might take the wrong way, so I do what my Mom says to do when you're trying to get a civilized conversation going. I ask her something about herself.

"Can I ask you something?"

"I guess so."

"Why do you dress like that?"

She has changed from her sailing outfit of shorts and a t-shirt back into her usual billowy skirts and a white cotton blouse.

Alyssum looks a little surprised, but then she answers, "Because of wants and needs."

"What?"

171

"It's a long story."

"Why you dress the way you do is a long story?"

"Yeah. It has to do with my parents' life philosophy. Like I said, it has to do with wants and needs."

"I don't get it."

"Mom and Dad believe that it's bad to spend too much money on things we just want instead of things we really need."

"But you have a lot of stuff in your room."

"Well, like I said, I want to be a scientist or a vet, and since my school is in my house, I have stuff that other kids would get to use at school."

"Like the telescope?"

"Yeah. It's like since you are a writer, you need a dictionary."

"What does that have to do with your clothes?"

"I like bright-coloured clothes and I like to change about six times a day, but I don't really *need* to own all new stuff, or designer jeans. That would be kind of greedy. For the price of one pair of jeans, I can buy twenty second-hand outfits from garage sales or the church thrift shop."

"Do you like wearing old clothes?"

"Sure. It's fun to have so many crazy clothes to choose from. We do have a washing machine and a sewing machine, so it's not like I'm wearing other people's dirty old clothes."

"Oh." It all sounds a bit strange. I wonder what things I *really* need, as opposed to all the stuff I want to have. Or, want to do. Like, do I really *need* a bus ticket to Ontario, or is that just being greedy?

"My parents also believe that if you're lucky enough to have more than you need, you should share."

"Like taking the leftovers from the market to the old age home?"

Alyssum nods but she doesn't seem very interested

in talking about wants and needs any more. It's like she has a handy little set speech ready for when people ask and doesn't like to say any more about it. I sure wish I'd asked her earlier.

I try to think of another question. The stress level definitely goes down when we're talking.

"What did your dad mean about getting help with a project?"

Alyssum looks a little pained and I wonder if I've blown it by asking the wrong question.

"Well, there are two reasons I need help. One is that Dad thought if I had someone to work with, I'd be more likely to stick with it. And, since this is a really important project, I have to keep going no matter what."

Listening to her, I'm getting a little worried. Whatever it is she's talking about sounds like a lot of work.

"And the other problem is I really need someone to help me . . . someone who can write."

We both look at my stacks of reference books, the jar stuffed full of pens on the bedside table, my notebooks. . . .

"I guess I should have thought of you before."

"Well, tell me—what's your project?"

I've never seen anyone look the way Alyssum does. She seems less agitated and her eyes warm with excitement. She starts bouncing gently on the bed.

"You know, you might actually like doing this project." She bounces a bit faster.

I still have no clue what she's thinking, but there's something contagious about how she nods at me, like she's expecting me to agree. I'm so curious now, there's no way I can resist and so, I nod back.

"Tell me!"

Alyssum talks and I listen. It doesn't take long before I know that I *do* want to help her. For the next half-hour we are lost in a flurry of plans and ideas. I make notes and draw diagrams. The more we talk, the more I realize how stupid I've been. It's strange, though—the longer we go on, scheming and plotting, the less I feel a need to do more apologizing or formal "making up."

By the time Mom calls up the stairs to say it's time for the Cranwells to go, it's like we never had any kind of fight at all. I want to ask if Alyssum can stay a little longer. If Granny and Grandpa hadn't been here, I probably would have. As it is, we shake hands firmly at my bedroom door and agree to meet again as soon as possible.

Mom and Mrs. Cranwell exchange knowing glances at the bottom of the stairs, but my head is so full of plans I don't even feel like getting mad at them.

"Oh. I nearly forgot." Alyssum turns and comes back up the stairs. She pulls something out of a pocket hidden in the folds of her skirt and hands it to me. Then she turns and runs to join her parents who have already gone outside.

I turn over the handmade card. The paper is unmistakably from Tonya Windwoman's stand, soft and textured and a very pale shade of violet. Summer Lilac.

I read the message inside. "Happy Birthday and Welcome to Tarragon Island! Your friend, Alyssum."

I run down the stairs and join my family on the front steps where we wave goodbye to the Cranwells as they walk down our driveway. Alyssum looks back at us and waves crazily. When they all disappear around the bend, I invite Granny to come and see Dove Cottage.

"I can keep my new journal here," I say, putting the beautiful copper journal on my makeshift desk. It's a gift from my parents. Alyssum must have told them about it. "I'm going to get a desk in here one of these days—the boxes are only temporary," I say.

"Do you like it here?" Granny asks suddenly.

I pause before answering. Not so long ago I wouldn't have hesitated. I would have begged her to take me back with her. But with Granny standing right beside me, my trip to Guelph doesn't seem so desperately important.

"Well, I really, really miss you and Grandpa," I confess, "and my friends and my old school." I think of my room, the plaque on the shelf, and I think about my wants and needs. "There are things here I couldn't do in Ontario," I grudgingly admit.

"Like sailing?"

I have to say, the sailboat race was a lot of fun despite my silent feud. If we ever go sailing again, which I guess we will, we'll have even more fun. I don't say anything to Granny about my conversation with Alyssum and our new project. It's so new and exciting I don't want to spoil it by talking.

"Let me tell you a little story," Granny says. She looks around for an extra chair.

"You sit on the chair—I'll sit down here on the blanket." I feel like I'm swelling up with happiness. My Granny knows a thousand stories, and I love hearing them all. No summer would be complete without her familiar voice beginning in the familiar way.

"Once upon a time, there was a very wise king. He ruled gently and kindly and all his subjects adored him. He was also a man who felt deeply—when the rains didn't come and the crops failed, his people starved. When tragedy came to his land, he wept and wept.

"When things were going well, the sun shone and the crops flourished, he was consumed with the kind of joy that makes people sing and dance and celebrate."

"Can I come in?"

It's Matt. He has a sixth sense about Granny and

her stories. He hates to miss them. He waits until I open the door and then joins me down on the floor on the blanket.

"It's about a king," I whisper.

"I know. I was listening outside."

He squirms to the side when I poke him in the ribs, but then we both look up at Granny so she'll keep going.

"When things were going wrong and he was feeling terrible, the old king wanted to find a way to make himself feel better. He also wanted something to remind him that when things were going well, he shouldn't feel too smug, that he should always remain humble for his fortunes could change at any time."

Granny pauses and looks around the rustic inside of Dove Cottage. "This is a lovely place to write, Heather," she says.

"Then what happens, Granny?" Matt asks.

"The old king called the wisest woman in his kingdom to come and visit him and he asked her to find him something that would make him feel better when he was feeling miserable and would keep him humble when things were going well. The old crone agreed to try and help and she set off to search the kingdom for a solution to the king's dilemma.

"The woman travelled far away for many, many weeks and when she finally returned, she handed the king a small box."

"What was in it?" Matt asks. I poke him in the ribs again, this time to make him keep quiet.

"There was a ring in the box. A plain, gold band. The king took the ring out of the box and held it up to the light, which is when he noticed that there were four words engraved into the gold."

"What did it say?"

Matt can never wait for the ending of the story.

"Be quiet! Let Granny finish."

She draws in her breath and very solemnly says, "This, too, shall pass."

Outside the door, I hear the flutter of wings as a bird lands in the grass outside the door and then flies away again.

Granny smiles at me and reaches forward to touch my hair. "The only thing we know for sure in this life is that things change. The friends you left in Toronto are a whole summer older and are different than when you left. New people live in your old house. Nothing stays the same."

I cringe inside and think of the North Hill Writing Group. I know Granny is right, but I don't want to nod.

"Matt, honey. Could you give us a minute alone?"

For once, Matt doesn't say anything. "Sure. Thanks for the story, Granny."

"And don't you be listening outside the door. I'll meet you at Barnaby's pen in a few minutes. I understand your mother will need a hand taking off those bandages."

We listen to Matt's feet swishing through the grass.

"Heather, your grandfather and I would like to give you a private present."

"A private present?"

She passes me a plain white envelope.

"Well go ahead, open it."

"Oh, Granny." I don't know what else to say. Inside the envelope is a cheque for seventy-five dollars, exactly enough for a bus ticket to Ontario.

"You may use that for whatever you like as long as you consider all your options and make a good decision."

My cheeks are hot with tears when I throw my arms around her neck. She holds me very gently and whispers, "This, too, shall pass."

Chapter Twenty-three

Collected Quote #61
I'd like to get away from earth awhile
And then come back to it and begin over.
May no fate willfully misunderstand me
And half grant what I wish and snatch me away
Not to return. Earth's the right place for love:
I don't know where it's likely to go better.
—Robert Frost, "Birches"
Source: one of Grandpa's favourite poems. Reminds him of
when he used to climb trees when he was a little boy.

September 4th—Dove Cottage
Today has been the absolute best day all summer. Granny and Grandpa took me into Victoria to buy school supplies! Ever since we got back I've been organizing my new binders and folders, sorting out my new pens, felts, coloured pencils, and notebooks.

I start school tomorrow, the same day Granny and Grandpa fly back to Ontario. It was a quick visit, but Grandpa doesn't like to be away from the farm for more than a few days. I have a plan, though. I've been showing them all over the island and telling them how it would be a great place to retire. At first, Grandpa said he would farm until the day he dropped, and then I pointed out that he could farm just as well here on the island.

He said he knew that in theory, but until a farmer walks the land he doesn't know for sure what kind of feelings he'll have about it. And, he says, a farmer has to feel good about a place before he'd consider moving. It seems to me like he and Granny are thinking about it. I hope I'm not being too pushy, I know it takes a little time to get used to the idea of moving someplace new.

If they decide not to move here, well, I have enough in my bank account to visit them, maybe at Christmas.

Two other great things happened today. One was that Barnaby has been flapping both his wings a lot since Mom took off the bandages and this morning, Matt said he saw Barnaby's feet lift off the ground. Mom says that means it won't be long now before we can set him free. The other great thing is that Mr. Turnbull liked the article I gave him! It wasn't exactly about poverty here on Tarragon Island, but he said sometimes the direction a story takes can change, and that's okay.

I can't believe I nearly forgot—something else great happened. Granny and I were at a garage sale and we found the perfect desk for Dove Cottage. We brought it home and painted it Summer Lilac. It fits perfectly under the window and is just the right size to go with my chair. That's where I'm writing now—in my journal with the copper cover.

Seeing my name on my article in the *Tarragon Times* is just as exciting the second time as it was the first. Mom and Dad bought twelve copies of the paper and I carefully cut out copies for Maggie, for Mr. Helliwell, my old Language Arts teacher, and one for Granny and Grandpa.

Before I fold the clipping into the envelope, I look over the article one more time and try to imagine what Granny and Grandpa will say when they read it together in the kitchen of the old farmhouse.

Wants, Needs and Sharing
by Heather Blake

Often, when looking at a mass of things for sale, he would say to himself, "How many things I have no need of."—Socrates

Last year, when I was twelve and lived in the big booming metropolis of Toronto, I used to think I needed many things that really aren't important. I thought my life would end without the new All Spice CD, Kelly Jeans and pedal pushers. Now, I'm a whole year older and a whole year wiser.

I have moved to Tarragon Island and met many great people and made some new friends, including Alyssum Cranwell. Alyssum has taught me to appreciate what I have and the difference between wants and needs. Even though Alyssum goes to school at home and is a couple of years younger than me, she sure knows a lot!

She told me about starving children in Africa and Asia who would love just one bowl of rice a day and a glass of clean, running water. These are the children who really have *needs*, not wants like us.

One day, when searching the Internet, Alyssum found out that some organizations such as C.A.R.E. and OXFAM Canada have programs to help children in third world countries who lead lives that even I can't imagine. Right then and there Alyssum decided to donate some of the profits from the hand-made soap she sells at the market each week to OXFAM and C.A.R.E.

Together Alyssum and I have formed a club for kids on Tarragon Island who are interested in helping to save the lives of millions of children in other countries. We need volunteers with good minds and good voices willing to help us with bottle drives, the UNICEF Halloween coin drive and a car wash. We need ideas and plans to help the Tarragon Island Kids Helping Kids Klub get off the ground. For more information, contact Alyssum or me.

Before I moved to Tarragon Island I had no idea how lucky I was to be well fed and cared for. Now I know. Please come to our first meeting on September 15th at Alyssum's house (call us if you don't know where that is) to find out more about why all of us on Tarragon are so lucky and how we can help others who aren't.

I lick the back of the envelope and close the flap on my story. Christmas isn't so far away and I'm sure we'll see Granny and Grandpa again. If I really get desperate, I've got my secret stash of money for a bus ticket, though I'm thinking I might use part of it to pay for photocopies of our Tarragon Island Kids Helping Kids Klub flyers.

Anyway, right now I don't really have time to make a trip. Alyssum and I have to be at the market every week until the season ends to hand out flyers.

Even though the paper just came out today, already two people who are interested in helping phoned me and another one called Alyssum. One of the phone calls was from a boy!

I've made two new friends at school and Mr. Turnbull told me about a creative writing class at the community centre. I signed up right away. We're supposed to bring part of a work in progress to read and discuss. It's strange, even though Alyssum is pretty rich, she has taught me a lot about poverty, so maybe I should get back to work on my novel about Rosie. I could take part of that to my first writing class.

Although, I've been thinking maybe I should start work on a new story. I have this idea for a novel about a girl whose parents get killed in a terrible train crash and she has to go and stay with this aunt she hardly knows. The aunt is very eccentric and lives on a sailboat and makes her living telling people's fortunes.

There are a lot of fortune-tellers here on Tarragon Island, not just the rune man. That's very handy because it makes it so much easier to do my research. . . .

About the Author

Nikki Tate is a writer and professional storyteller who is popular at library and school readings. She lives with her daughter Danielle on the Saanich Peninsula of British Columbia's beautiful Vancouver Island. Tate has chosen to set her novels for children in her familiar countryside and the nearby Gulf Islands. "My lovely garden and the glorious views of Mount Baker and the Gulf Islands are my biggest enemies! How am I supposed to get any work done when I live in such spectacular surroundings?"

Coming in the Spring of 2000!

MYSTERY ON TARRAGON ISLAND
by Nikki Tate

Adjusting to her family's move from Toronto to tiny Tarragon Island, British Columbia, has been difficult for aspiring writer Heather Blake. Thirteen-year-old Heather joins a creative writing class but instead of making friends and working on her novel about poverty and despair, she becomes embroiled in a real-life crime investigation! Meanwhile, she finds herself in competition with an arrogant mystery writer, and in the throes of puppy love.

Also by Nikki Tate . . . the Bestselling StableMates Series!

StableMates 1: Rebel of Dark Creek—Meet Jessa, a grade six girl from Vancouver Island, who falls in love with a pony named Rebel. Jessa must learn to juggle school, barn chores, and friendship in this story of determination and ingenuity.

StableMates 2: Team Trouble at Dark Creek—Two giant draft horses arrive at Dark Creek Stables, and Jessa's pony, Rebel, finds himself out in the cold during the worst blizzard of the century. To complicate matters, Jessa and her best friend, Cheryl, have an argument, and an unexpected visitor almost ruins Jessa's Christmas vacation.

StableMates 3: Jessa Be Nimble, Rebel Be Quick—As an eventing clinic draws closer, Jessa needs to find a way to conquer her fears about water jumps. At school she's assigned to help Midori, a new student from Japan, settle in. Cheryl is no help at all—she's too busy trying to land a juicy part in a play.

StableMates 4: Sienna's Rescue—When four abused and neglected horses are seized by the Kenwood Animal Rescue Society, Jessa convinces Mrs. Bailey that Dark Creek Stables would be a perfect foster farm for one of them, but nobody is prepared for the challenges of Sienna's rehabilitation. Can Jessa and her friends save the young renegade mare from the slaughterhouse?

StableMates 5: Raven's Revenge—When Jessa wins a trip for two to horse camp, she and Cheryl are so excited they can hardly think of anything else. But Camp Singing Waters may not be a blissful getaway. Feuding campers, a lame horse and drafty cabins are bad enough, but should they have listened more carefully to Mrs. Bailey's ominous warning about Dr. Rainey's experiments with witchcraft? Or, are the late-night ghost stories around the campfire just fuelling their overactive imaginations?

StableMates 6: Return to Skoki Lake—Jessa's week-long trail riding trip into the Rocky Mountains should have been the experience of a lifetime. Ignoring increasingly peculiar symptoms, Jessa sets off into the mountains, determined to enjoy herself despite feeling very ill. To her horror, she finds herself regaining consciousness in an Alberta hospital bed! This is only the beginning of a long journey of recovery, one which turns Jessa's life upside down and threatens even her desire to ride.